The Cursed

Book Two in the Clandestine Series

by H.M. Kanicki

First paperback edition November 2019

Book design by H.M. Kanicki
Poem by William Shakespeare

ISBN 1694762777 (paperback)
Also available on Kindle

I dedicate this book to my best friend. Thank you for always being there for me. Here's to 30 more years of silly 80's lyrics and late-night talks.

Chapter 1

Marion Spaller's wise, gray eyes smiled at Elli and Justin
when they returned, hand in hand, to the central room of
Ravenwood. It was obvious that she knew what had transpired
between the girl with the forest green eyes and long, silky,
brunette hair and her grandson in the overlook, but kept silent
about the subject. Teddy and Cyn Dal tried to politely ignore
the change between their two friends by looking intently at a
large book they had removed from a box with a crest carved on
the top of it.

Only Page, a knowing smile on her pixie-like face, spoke
what she and the others were thinking, making her red curls
bounce with the movement. "It's about time."

With a little twitch at the corners of her mouth, the only
evidence of the delight she kept hidden, Marion waited
patiently for Elli and Justin to settle themselves on an empty
bench carved with blooming roses that looked so real that Elli
could almost smell their sweet scent.

"Now, child," Marion began after a moment's reflection,
"I need you to tell me everything. I want a complete listing of
all the premonitions you've had since you arrived at
Clandestine University."

Closing her eyes, Elli concentrated on remembering her premonitions, knowing in her heart that they were the key to saving Branda from the torturing Acolytes. "I remember something about a book with flipping pages and then a cave. I think the cave is Ravenwood because I had heard a voice say 'the Ravenwood will fly,' and then I saw the red clouds and lightning that we ran from. There were two hands. One was kind and one was cruel, almost grasping. And then there was something about a promise."

"A promise?" Justin asked, his voice soft. Opening her eyes, Elli saw a thoughtful look on his face.

"What is it?" she asked, but he remained silent as he wrapped his arms around her waist and pulled her closer.

"Is there anything else, child?" Marion's question drew Elli's attention away.

"I remember having one when we went through the lightning, but it still doesn't make any sense to me. There was a man in a strange costume with a ruffled collar. He was writing on a piece of paper with a quill pen."

"What was he writing?" Page asked, absently twirling a red curl around her finger while she listened intently to Elli.

"It was a number. Sixty-five. He wrote it constantly, but that wasn't the only time I had a premonition about him. I had a second one when I...." Elli couldn't finish her sentence. Chills swept up her arms, making goose bumps rise. Justin's warmth did little to comfort her.

"When you had visions of Branda," he finished for her, matter-of-factly. Not trusting herself to speak, Elli only nodded.

"I can tell that it was difficult, but we have to know," Teddy said, his brown eyes understanding.

"If she doesn't want to talk about it, she doesn't have to," Justin said, gruffly breaking in.

"But, Justin –"

"No," he said, cutting Page off with a glare. "You didn't see her up there. I had to hold her down or she would've really hurt herself. She looked like she was in so much pain." Elli didn't have to look at Justin's face to know the expression he wore. His jaw would be clenched, a fire would be burning in his eyes, and his features would be like chiseled granite. She could feel his anger through the tensing of his muscles.

"It's okay," she whispered, leaning her head back and looking into his eyes. "I can do this. I have to. Branda's counting on me."

Before Justin could argue, Elli moved out of the circle of his arms and closed her eyes again, trying to remember everything she could about the premonition.

"The man was sitting in the corner and he was angry at me for not figuring out what he meant by the number sixty-five. Branda was strapped to a table and people were beating her. I could feel every welt. There was something about a purple stone and a locked box in the dean's office. I remember black objects wrapped in dark cloaks." Opening her eyes, Elli looked to Marion for enlightenment. "What does it all mean?"

"I don't know, child. I'm sor–"

"Sixty-five!" Cyn Dal yelled, sitting straight up, her almond eyes bright. Five quizzical faces looked at her in astonishment. "Sixty-five! Don't you get it? A man in a ruffled collar with a quill pen?"

In one excited motion, she jumped up from where she was sitting and raced to the bookshelves. After several moments of looking, she pulled a fat, leather-bound book from the collection and set it on the table in front of Elli. "There's your answer," Cyn Dal said proudly, gesturing at the book.

"*The Complete Works of William Shakespeare*," Elli read aloud. Opening the book to the first page, her heart jumped in her throat. "That's him!" she exclaimed, pointing to a portrait on the title page. The caption under it read *William Shakespeare*. He was a bit younger than in her vision, but there was no question that the slightly balding man wearing the funny white collar was the same one looking up at her.

"You said he kept writing the number sixty-five," Cyn Dal said, paging through the text, her action eerily like the first premonition Elli had had when arriving at Clandestine. When

Cyn Dal finally found the page she was looking for, she turned the book back toward Elli.

Elli felt her heart quicken when she saw the lines of the poem. She tried to read the words but felt her throat closing. Justin, feeling her tense beside him, looked over her shoulder and began to read aloud from the page. She knew the lines already. She'd seen them enough in her mind, but hearing his deep voice reading them was still eerie.

Sonnet 65

Since brass, nor stone, nor earth, nor boundless sea,
But sad mortality o'ersways their power,
How with this rage shall beauty hold a plea,
Whose action is no stronger than a flower?
O how shall summer's honey breath hold out
Against the wrackful siege of batt'ring days,
When rocks impregnable are not so stout,
Nor gates of steel so strong, but Time decays?
O fearful meditation! where alack,
Shall Time's best jewel from Time's chest lie hid?
Or what strong hand can hold his swift foot back?
Or who his spoil of beauty can forbid?
O none, unless this miracle have might,
That in black ink my love may still shine bright.

When Justin's voice stopped, the sound rang through the hall like the last phrase of a haunting melody.

"What does it mean?" Page finally asked, unable to stand the uncomfortable silence the poem had enshrouded them all in.

"I'm not sure, but it seems like such a depressing poem," Cyn Dal said, picking the book up and examining the words more closely.

"So, there's no hope?" Page questioned.

"How do we even know this is what the premonition meant?" Justin asked, defensively. "Cyn Dal could be wrong."

"She's not," Elli said, her voice hollow to her own ears.

"How can you be so sure?"

"Because some of the lines in the poem were in other premonitions I had. In fact, I started having them the very first night that I came to Clandestine University," Elli replied, meeting Justin's eyes.

"But I don't see how this poem is going to help us save Branda," Teddy pointed out, taking the book from Cyn Dal in his large, chocolate-colored hands and laying it back on the table. "It only talks about rocks and nature. It doesn't give us a clue as to how to get her back."

"Maybe it isn't talking about helping Branda," Cyn Dal said. "Maybe it's about the last battle. *Against the wrackful siege of batt'ring days.* Those days are now."

"I think you're right," Marion said, her voice resigned. "Perhaps Shakespeare was a descendent of Merlin. Many famous and exceptional people throughout history were. I can see no reason why he should be any different. He could have foreseen the words in a vision."

"Or maybe he overdosed on opium," Justin said, scornfully. "This isn't bloody English class. We've got to get Branda out of Clandestine. If Elli is right, she doesn't have much time. I say we skip the tutorial and start thinking for ourselves."

"But what about the rest of her vision?" Page asked. "We can't go in almost blind. We've got to know more. Elli dreamed about a crystal. The poem says, 'Time's best jewel.' I think it's referring to Merlin's crystal that's been hidden for millennia. She also saw a locked box in the dean's office. Maybe that box holds a key to finding the crystal."

As Elli sat, listening to her friends, she let her mind drift. It seemed odd to her that only a short time ago she'd had a relatively normal life. Keeping out of her Great-Uncle Ambrose's way and coming up with a topic to write her term paper on were the most critical things she worried about. At least they were until she came to Clandestine University, which just happened to have its very own band of soul-stealing Acolytes who dream of ruling the world through black, elemental magic.

Now she, who, according to an ancient book, was some kind of mystical chosen one that had the ability to control all four elements, and her friends, the descendants of who else but Merlin, were the only ones to stand in their way. Not to mention it was very possible that her death was the only thing may restore the balance between good and evil; otherwise the world would be thrown into eternal chaos.

But the best part of the whole ordeal was that the only clues to winning this fight came from her uncontrollable premonitions and a sonnet from a guy who had been dead for a few hundred years. *Boy*, Elli thought, not even trying to squelch the sarcasm running through her mind, *this is going to be a piece of cake.*

Lost in her thoughts, Elli found that it became more and more difficult to concentrate on what Justin and the others were saying. The room seemed to fade around her; the soft candle and fire light began to blur until they were little more than blobs of dancing fuzziness. She had very little sensation of her body or where she sat, but seemed to float free, suspended outside herself. It was then that she heard the whispers.

Unsure of what to do as this was unlike any kind of premonition she'd ever had, Elli felt her head turn as she tried to decipher what was being said. It sounded like a single word being repeated over and over again. Straining, she was finally able to pick it out. "See... see... see..." The whispering grew louder until it was almost shouting. "See... see... *see!*"

Stars exploded behind Elli's eyes and she felt herself falling. Not off the bench but into herself. Into her mind. It was like pitching over the side of a well and seeing her surroundings fade into the distance as she plummeted down.

Pictures began to form in her mind, highly detailed images that were more vivid than any other premonition she'd ever had. She saw herself standing in front of a mirror that shimmered around the edges in every color of the rainbow, like the iridescence on a soap bubble. Gazing at her own reflection, she realized that the mirror wasn't made of glass. It was water.

As she stood there pondering how a pool of water could stay upright without spilling over the mirror frame's lip, she saw her image begin to change. Her long, brown hair began to grow longer and become silvery white. Her green eyes became a brilliant aquamarine. They seemed so much older than seventeen. Ancient and wise and, yet, somber as well. Her clothing shifted until she was wearing a gown with billowing sleeves that seemed to be made of the water, itself. Small marine life seemed to swim over the surface of the gown, yet it moved like cloth.

Though transfixed by the image, it dawned on Elli that she wasn't staring at herself but at another person who was on the other side of the mirror. A name formed in her mind. *The Lady of the Lake.* The pale head gave a single nod to confirm Elli's thought. It didn't seem strange that this mystical reflection was able to read her mind. Speech just felt wrong in her presence.

"God-daughter, child of Merlin, you must find it before it's too late." The Lady's voice was like sea spray in Elli's mind, and it made all her unanswered questions bob to the surface of her thoughts. What do you want? How is any of this possible? How did you find me? Is what Marion said true? Why me?

It was obvious that the Lady understood Elli's thoughts, but she raised a gentle hand as if to stop her questions and then smiled sadly before continuing, *"I have little time. Know only that what you are seeing is a memory given to you at birth, and that it is simply playing out at the appointed time."*

"But how can you give someone a memory at birth?"

"Water is water, God-daughter," the Lady said mysteriously. *"But that is not important. Merlin bade me watch over his child, and I have done so. God-daughter, you must restore the Army of Light to full power and complete your*

destiny."

"I don't understand. Please!" Elli's watched as the Lady raised one pale hand and pointed to something off to Elli's right. Turning her head, she saw a window appear before her and pictures begin to flash by. She saw herself, standing alone with her back to blackness. Cupped in her hands was an object that glowed an enigmatic purple color. Though the object was small, it seemed to pulse with a powerful life.

"Find the crystal, child. You have no time to waste. You must complete your destiny. Restore the army. Follow the lines. The answer is in the words."

Unable to pull her eyes from the glowing crystal, Elli cried frantically, *"Please, I'm so afraid. How can I save everyone? I'm only a girl."*

"If you doubt yourself, then this war has already been lost. You must choose, God-daughter. You must make the choice to follow your destiny or to flee from it. It is not an easy decision to make. So much depends on you, but you must choose. You cannot proceed until you do. My time is done."

Turning back toward the image of the Lady, Elli felt dismay. She saw the Lady fading away into the rainbow-colored water. *"What is my destiny? What do I do with the crystal once I have it?"*

"Choose," the Lady whispered.

Elli watched as the Lady slowly disappeared, her watery dress swirling around her. *"Please, Godmother!"* she exclaimed, reaching out her hands to grab the fading image. *"What do I do? Where do I look?"*

As soon as Elli touched the watery-mirror, she felt herself sucked in. Black, choking water surrounded her on all sides. Her lungs burned for the breath that was denied them, and her arms and legs seemed like weights, pulling her down.

Panic filled her chest and Elli sensed malevolent eyes watching her, laughing at her pain. Desperately clawing through the water, trying to out swim the dizziness that was taking over, Elli saw a wavy image of a locked box before her, suspended in the water. Reaching towards it, her oxygen-deprived brain grasping at straws, Elli saw a cruel hand coming at her, leaving a trail of bloody water in its wake. Opening her mouth to scream, she felt the water pour into her mouth and down her throat. The hand closed around her....

Chapter 2

Elli bolted from her seat, screaming, fear-sweat covering her.

"Elli, it's okay! You're safe." The voice sounded panicked to Elli's hypersensitive ears. Opening her eyes, she found herself in Justin's arms. The expression on his face was a cross between worry over her and anger at whatever had made her react the way she did.

The smell of wood smoke and pine was strong to her sensitive nose, and the light of the candles seemed extraordinarily bright. Puzzled and unsure of what had happened, she looked away from Justin toward her friends who had shocked looks on their faces. Then she looked at Marion. Justin's grandmother sat in her wheelchair, her gray eyes intense.

When Elli noticed the woman's hand outstretched toward her with concern, she remembered everything. The room swam around her, and she could see the disembodied hand again, its image imprinted over everything like a photo with double-exposure. It seemed to rush at her like a shark, the talon-like nails making her think of teeth. Before she could react, it reached her. As soon as it made contact, Elli felt her heart beat strangely and her knees buckle. Her eyes closed of their own accord, her body went numb, and her breath caught in her throat. Darkness filled her senses.

***

"Elli!" Justin could hear the shocked fear in his own voice as he called her name. He barely heard the collective shout of alarm from his friends. Pulling Elli closer to him, Justin felt her body give several small shudders before it went limp and still as a doll's. Panic filled him. "Gran, she's not moving!"

With a quick gesture of her hand, Marion pointed toward the large table in the room. "Lay her over there. Teddy, push me closer," she fairly commanded. "Page, get my kit and a bowl of water." The red-head rushed off to get them.

Lifting Elli into his arms, Justin carried her to the table and laid her head on the pillow Cyn Dal had provided. He felt his stomach clench as he realized how shallow Elli's breathing was. "She's barely breathing!" he exclaimed. His insides were doing somersaults and his hands were shaking.

He watched as his gran took her kit, a small wooden box with a cross etched into the top, from Page's hand. She took from it a few dried holly berries which she rubbed between her fingers. Her eyes began to transform from their usual gray to a piercing green color, almost as if an inner light had been turned on. It would have been surprising if he wasn't so used to it; all elemental's eyes changed color when they connected with their magic.

Gran placed her hands on Elli's forehead, as if she was checking for a fever. Wondering if she had one, Justin touched Elli's cheek. Her skin felt oddly chilled; taking her hand in his, he knew his own eyes changed to red as he tried to send his body heat into her.

"She's still partly in some kind of vision," Cyn Dal said anxiously, taking the bowl of water from Page and laying it on the table beside Elli's still form. "Do you think she's being attacked?"

"Attacked?" Justin snapped, anger bubbling in his veins.

After several torturous seconds, Gran raised her still-glowing eyes and Justin felt her penetrating gaze. "It's more like she's being debilitated. They aren't trying to kill her, only keep her from getting farther away from them."

Justin didn't need her to explain who the 'they' were. Kneeling beside Elli, he stroked her hair gently and whispered in her ear, "Fight them, love. I can't lose you. I just found you. Please, fight." He felt his heart contract.

It had been so long since he'd let himself feel love that it unnerved him. Love always came with fear attached to it, the big "what if". Anger was easier. And now, he used that anger to give him strength. If he let himself collapse at the thought of losing her... he *wouldn't* lose her.

He reached for her in his mind and though finding her silent almost made him crack, he simply sent warmth and strength to her, hoping it would do her some good.

The scent of vanilla bean and lavender made him look to his gran again. She was carefully adding them to the small basin of water. Then, with deft fingers, she soaked a small towel in the water, rang it out, and then laid on Elli's forehead.

"Teddy, this will take the both of us," she urged. The boy immediately stepped forward, his eyes already changing to the same brilliant green as Marion's. With anxiety like a rock in his stomach, Justin watched as they both silently reached for their magic.

***

In a small corner of her mind that the grasping hand didn't quite reach, Elli became aware of a dim light that was fighting through the darkness that smothered her. Reaching for it, she sensed Justin's warmth and strength coming toward her like tendrils of smoke under a closed door. She embraced them and felt a small part of her wake up.

She heard his voice calling to her as if from a great
distance, begging her to fight. She'd never heard him use that
tone of voice before, and it left her feeling afraid, more afraid
than anything she'd seen so far. She listened to Justin's voice.
Elli made herself fight against the hand's crushing grip. She
could feel its nails digging into her, and she mentally screamed
with pain and determination. It felt like a thousand ice picks
were poking her at once. Or like the hand was slowly peeling
the skin from her body, strip by strip. She knew it would stop
hurting if she gave up. If she gave in....

This realization only made her want to fight more. As
she struggled, new sensations came to her like light through
horizontal blinds. A cloth felt cold on her flushed face. The
smell of vanilla and lavender was strong as she sensed two
pairs of hands hovering over her.

Behind her eyes, a green light began to grow and fill the
nightmare-coated places of her brain, forcing the fingers of the
evil hand to loosen their hold on her one-by-one. An
overwhelming peace filled her and coerced the last of the evil
to leave her.

It became easier to breathe and the pain vanished. She
could feel Justin's love not just as small smoke tendrils but
fully and completely. Her eyes no longer seemed quite so
heavy and fluttered open to see Marion and Teddy standing
over her, a green light surrounding them. Lifting one of her
hands in amazement, Elli found herself covered in the same
greenish-glow. It was then that the light faded, and Teddy and
Marion lowered their arms. Elli watched in amazement as their
glowing green eyes returned to their normal color.

"Elli," Justin's voice said her name like a prayer. His
gray eyes, a tinge of red fading from the irises, met her gaze.
Taking her hand in his and kissing it ever so gently, he asked,
"Are you okay?"

"I think so," Elli croaked, her voice sounding rough and
scratchy to her own ears despite the wonderfully lightness she
felt.

A relieved smile spread across his face only to be

replaced with a strained one. "Don't ever do that to again." Squeezing his hand weakly, Elli tried to sit up only to have Justin press her gently back down. "I think you should rest," he said. "You've been through a lot."

"And she'll have been through a lot more before things are done." Marion's voice, though soft, was filled with a quiet determination that pulled Elli's gaze from Justin. The old woman sat in her wheelchair surrounded by the others, her wise, gray eyes cloudy with dismay. "You were locked in a vision, child. What did you see?"

"Can't it wait?" Justin asked, his voice gruff with annoyance.

"Justin," Elli said, squeezing his hand a little more strongly this time and then forcing her limp muscles to raise her into a sitting position, the now-dry cloth falling into her lap. Ignoring how the room dipped and swayed to her dizzy mind, Elli forced herself to give a level gaze to each person. "Marion's right. We've got work to do."

***

"I don't care what you say. We can't go back in the same door that Elli and I came out of. They'll have it barricaded or under guard. Either way, they'll suspect us to try and come in that way." Justin's voice rang angrily off the stone walls of the Ravenwood living area, a schematic of Clandestine University spread out on the table.

Running a hand through her freshly washed hair, Elli sighed. It had seemed like such an easy proposition last night, sitting by the fire with her friends at her side, relating the story of how she'd just met her godmother, the mystical Lady of the Lake, in a vision. Of course, she'd left out the part about how it was really a memory the Lady had given her and how she'd almost drowned in it.

They'd only ask her a ton of questions that she couldn't answer. Besides, Justin would have packed her up and left the country before she would've had a chance to tell him her plan –

to break into Clandestine University, save Branda and steal some kind of box from the demonic dean's office. Simple? Hardly since no one knew how to go about it.

"Look. According to these plans that Cyn Dal found on the computer, there's no other way into the place aside from scaling the tower walls and I don't know about you, but I'm not exactly James Bond," Page said, gesturing at the schematic.

"There has to be a way," Justin said, rubbing the back of his neck. "It's just that if we go in that way, we'll be caught in a second."

"But we don't even know where Branda is. Who says she's even in Clandestine?" Teddy asked. "All we have to go on is a vision of her being tortured. There's no other reference."

"No," Elli said, speaking for the first time, "she's there. I can feel it. I just don't know where."

"Well, you were only there for two days. It isn't like you had a ton of time to get to know it by heart," Cyn Dal added.

"Okay, what about climbing through some of the lower windows?" Page asked. "One of them has to be open, right? We just crawl right through and then find Branda."

"Yeah, but like Teddy said. Where? Clandestine is too big a place to just pick a random window to break into," Cyn Dal explained, peering over Justin's shoulder to look at the blueprint again.

"What about Elli? Why can't she try and have a vision about Branda again?" Page asked.

"Absolutely not," Justin began, glaring at Page. "It's too dangerous. We barely got her out of the last one."

"I don't have any control over them. My premonitions don't work that way," Elli added with a frown, feeling useless.

"But why can't they? I mean the visions come from you. It's like hearing a song that you haven't heard in a long time and it springing a memory that you'd totally suppressed. I once knew this girl who would connect songs with her ex-boyfriends. She'd be okay and then all of a sudden, a song would come on the radio and she'd get real sad thinking about him and –"

"Page," Cyn Dal said, with a laugh. "Come up for breath."

"Amongst all of that, I think there was the start of a brilliant idea," Marion said, sitting forward in her chair.

"There was?" Justin asked roughly, receiving a scowl from his red-headed friend.

"Yes. Elli, look at the blueprint. Maybe something will trigger a vision like Page said," Marion explained, her expression hopeful.

Feeling her throat close, Elli nodded a reply and pulled the schematic closer. Her heart began to beat rapidly with anxiety. *What if I can't do this? What if it doesn't work? I've never tried to make myself have a premonition. I'll let everyone down. I'll let Branda down. I can't –* Elli's rant was cut off by a voice in her mind that felt like the gentle caress of rose petals to her frantic thoughts.

"*Child, have a little faith in yourself,*" Marion said. "*You wouldn't be here if there was no hope.*"

"*We all believe in you. Give it a try. We can't be in any worse shape for trying,*" Page said, a cool breeze in Elli's mind. It was a strange feeling to have so many people in her mind at once, like changing your clothes in the middle of a crowd. No privacy even though the voices were friendly and tried to be unobtrusive. Page's telepathic voice was seconded by Teddy and Cyn Dal, leaving the sensation of rain falling on leaves in her brain.

Odd, she thought, *how their elements are connected when they speak together.* Blushing a little at the thought that they might hear her, Elli felt a little more confidence creep into her. At least she did until she realized that there was one voice that she hadn't heard.

"Justin," she whispered, looking up to find him staring angrily at the wall behind her, his arms crossed.

"I'd be lying if I said I was thrilled about this," he said between clenched teeth. Then, like steam being released, his body relaxed in exasperation and he threw up his arms. "But I can't think of any other way." Looking down at her, his eyes a mix of emotions, he said, softly, "Just be careful."

With a small smile and a reassuring telepathic message, Elli closed her eyes and took several calming breaths. Only when her hands weren't shaking did she look once more at the blueprint. Reaching out, she let her palms hover over the image, moving them ever so slightly from one section to another. When her little fingers began to tingle and her heart skipped a beat, Elli quickly let her hands fall on the area she was over. The instant that she made contact, she was bombarded with visions that flooded her mind with sensations.

Branda. Lying on a cold, stone floor. Diamond windows. Torches. Blood. Pain. Laughter. Diamond windows. Chains clinking. Pyramid. Children. Diamond windows....

As suddenly as the images came, they went, leaving Elli tense and breathing heavily. The paper under her hands was rough to her fingers, reminiscent of the wood it was born of. Her eyes hurt from the brightness of the candles on the table, and the smell of burnt vanilla-scented wax was strong. Justin's hands on her shoulders were warm through her shirt though she didn't remember him moving to her side.

"Are you all right, child?" Marion asked, setting a cup of strong mint tea in front of Elli who, gratefully, drank every drop before speaking.

"I'm fine." Elli's voice sounded funny to her own, highly sensitive ears. "Where were my hands when I went in?"

"Over the old section of the school. It's condemned. They even had it barricaded so no one can get in," Cyn Dal said, filling Elli's cup.

"I've been there before." Elli quickly drained the cup again and sat back.

"When?" Teddy asked.

"The night before we ran away. I was there –," Elli paused, quickly glancing up at Justin who had resumed his post on the other side of the table when he'd been sure she was okay, "exploring. I had a vision of diamond-patterned windows that I remember seeing in that area." Though she wasn't sure why she'd quickly changed her story, Elli was amazed that no one seemed to notice the slight pause.

"Okay, so we know where to look. Now what? What about the crystal that the Lady talked about? How do we go about finding that?" Page inquired, playing with the corner of the blueprint.

"I have a feeling that the answer is in that box I keep seeing. Maybe it holds some kind of map or directions or Merlin's second book," Elli replied, biting her lower lip as she thought.

"Whatever it contains, I don't think we're going to have a chance of coming back to Ravenwood after we get Branda out," Teddy added. "Maybe we should be making some long-term plans, too."

"That sounds wise," Marion said. "In Elli's vision, the Lady seemed very anxious that you begin the search for Merlin's stone right away. The Acolytes aren't going to be pleased about losing their prisoner, and you may not get a second chance to find it if you return here."

"But, what about you?" Page asked. "They might come here." The sound of fear in Page's voice made Elli's stomach tighten.

"I don't think they can. No one can come into Ravenwood without permission, and I'm not so old and daft that I'd let someone in if I didn't know them."

"I didn't mean...." Page replied, leaving the sentence unfinished.

"I know, child. You didn't mean to upset me, and I appreciate your concern, but I'll be fine. You and the others will have enough to worry about."

"Aren't we putting too much faith on a box that no one has looked inside? For all we know, it could be old love letters," Justin interrupted, cynically.

"We've got to try. It's the only lead we have," Cyn Dal said, crossing her arms and leaning back in her chair.

"But that still leaves us with the issue of getting Branda

out of Clandestine," Justin added.

"I've got an idea," Elli said, giving him a meaningful look.

After a pause, Justin saw her plan form inside his mind, and he didn't like it one bit. "Oh, no. There's no way I'm going to let you do that. Not in a million years. Forget it, love."

Chapter 3

"This is absolutely ridiculous. I can't believe she talked me into this." Justin had been muttering to himself for the entire ride back to Clandestine University, his hands tense where he gripped the steering wheel of the van he'd borrowed from a farmer he'd befriended years ago, as his old car had not survived their first escape from the Acolytes. The more he grumbled, the angrier he got. "This plan has got to be the worst one in history."

"You wouldn't be saying that if you'd thought of it first," Elli said, determined that he wouldn't talk her out of it. She looked out the van window and refused to look at him. She was afraid he'd see that she wasn't as confident as she was pretending to be.

"If I'd thought of it, I'd be checking myself into a sanitarium right about now."

"You said yourself that we couldn't get back in through the secret passage since they'd be watching it. You said there was no other way," Elli replied.

"Yeah, but that doesn't mean I have to like it," he complained, gripping the steering wheel a little more tightly, his knuckles white with frustration.

The plan. It was so simple that Elli couldn't believe she hadn't thought of it before the vision. The images of a pyramid and small children had given her the idea, reminding her of the time she'd lived with her parents in Cairo. She'd practically lived on the shore of the Nile that year, playing with her friends in the shade of the palm trees while her parents taught at the university during the week and helped a good friend and colleague at his dig on the weekends. One day, while playing, Elli's friends found a snake sunning itself. Wanting to catch it, one boy, more daring than the others, picked up a stick and started smacking the ground in front of it, drawing the snake's attention. Another child circled around and picked it up by the tail and then dropped it into a bucket.

Why not a surprise attack? Justin was right. *They* couldn't get back through the secret passage, but maybe she could. If she walked right up to the front door and offered herself in place of Branda, the Acolytes would know that something was up. But if she crept in like she was going to rescue her friend, maybe they'd think she was just stupid to try a way they knew about. The Acolytes would take her right to Branda. *If the snake doesn't bite me first*, Elli thought, but quickly squelched it. The last thing she needed was for Justin to overhear her thoughts and add more fuel to the fire, so to speak.

It hadn't been easy to convince Justin to go along with Elli putting herself in danger. Trying to convince a forest fire to sway its course isn't a simple thing to do. It hadn't been until Elli said she wasn't going in alone and the others made the point that they had no other options that he'd finally gone along with it – that and a promise that she'd never do this again. While Elli was working her way down the not-so-secret passage, Justin and Teddy would be busy making a distraction so that when the signal came, Elli and Branda could escape. Cyn Dal and Page, however, would be breaking into the dean's office and stealing whatever they could carry, including the mysterious box. *Simple, right? God, what are we getting ourselves into?*

"We're nearly there. Get ready to throw open the door and make a run for it as soon as I stop." Justin sounded so matter-of-fact about the idea that Elli had a sudden feeling that they were going to succeed – or she did until he added, "I still don't like this but since I know I'm going to lose the argument, all I'll say is this. Be careful, love, and come back to me in one piece."

As the van pulled up at the bottom of the hill, Elli gave Justin a quick kiss on the lips, a savage smile that said she was looking forward to this, told her friends in the back seat 'good luck,' and jumped out the door. She waited a few moments for the van to race around the corner and out of sight, her heart jumping crazily in her chest at the thought of what she was about to do, and then started climbing up the hill that she and Justin had raced down only days ago.

The muscles in Elli's legs burned as she ascended, but her mind was too full of what she had to do to care. *Get inside. Wait for them to find me. Get taken to Branda. Give a signal. Run like mad. Ah, this is so easy. How can it fail?*

When she reached the top of the hill, it took her a minute to find the door. With only the moon as an aid, Elli ran her hands over the rough wood, trying to find a latch or a handle. After a few moments of futility, she sighed heavily, cursing in her mind. *It must open from the inside.* Closing her eyes, she let her mind drift back over what Marion had said before Elli and her friends had left for Clandestine.

***

The look that the girl in the mirror gave Elli wasn't exactly reassuring. Her green eyes were anxious, and her face was creased with worry. Too many things could go wrong tonight. Turning from the image, Elli hastily began to put on a pair of hiking boots she'd borrowed from Cyn Dal, knowing that their added warmth would be needed when they raided the old stone university, her hands shaking so much that she could barely tie the laces.

"Child?" a soft voice said from the door. Looking up, Elli found Marion entering the room, her wheelchair pushed by Teddy. With a smile and a nod, he departed, leaving Marion and Elli to their talk.

"Please sit," the old woman said, gesturing toward the chaise lounge that was against the wall near the door, her gaze steady. Once Elli was sitting, Marion took several deep breaths before speaking again, "The Fates have decreed that your adventure begin before you've been trained. I am sorry for that. If dealing with the Acolytes and ancient magic wasn't enough, you've got to do it without even knowing how to handle the power that flows through your veins."

The woman's words seemed to confirm Elli's worst fears. "So, there's no hope?" she asked, letting her eyes drop.

"No, child. There is always hope. Your instincts are sharp, and you've done very well. After all, you not only made yourself and my grandson invisible through the shifting of air, you were able to shield everyone in the car when the Acolytes struck through fire magic. You saved yourself and the only chance against the army of darkness by pure intuition."

"Is that what happened that day?" Elli's heart skipped a beat, and her eyes were wide with shock. "But I didn't even know what I was doing!"

"Yes, or who you are. Now that you know, I have every faith that you will discover your other powers. I've come to help you as best I can in this short time we have. Perhaps it will be enough for you to fight back, but no matter what happens, child, trust your instincts."

Unsure of how helpful her instincts had really been so far, she ran her hands up and down her arms, trying to fight the chill that suddenly enveloped her. "I think I understand," she replied, her voice calm despite the anxiety she was feeling. "So, what do I have to do?"

"I suppose I should explain a few things first. Elementals receive their magic from the things around them. We can't just wave a wand and conjure up a spell. We have to borrow magic from what's there. For example, earth elementals take their powers from the soil and from growing things. When Teddy and I heal someone, we use the natural magic from the herbs that are mixed in, let's say, a poultice. We encourage the healing parts of the plants to unfold and speed recovery. Though we cannot undo something that occurs naturally," Marion looked down at her own, blanket-covered legs to emphasize her point, "or force one magic to become another, we can make suggestions to plants to make them grow under unusual circumstances." Marion raised her hand and pointed to the flowering morning glories and heather growing on Elli's bed.

"But what about the lightning? You said that I stopped it. How? And if Justin is a fire elemental, why didn't he stop it?"

"I cannot answer your first question, child, I am sorry. However, I can give you some peace of mind about the second. Justin would have stopped that lightening if he could, but as a rule, elementals cannot control the weapons of others. He could not draw on the heat from the lightening any more than I can walk. The only defense an elemental has against another is diverting their power. Justin had no source of fire strong enough to handle the powers of all the Acolytes combined. It would have taken more than the strike of a match or the flame of a lighter."

Giving Elli a reassuring smile, and a pat on the arm, she continued, "Now your power, my girl, may be the exception to many rules. All that I know about elemental magic comes from those who possessed a single element. You, however, contain all four. As I've said, it is impossible to change one element into another, but maybe you did something else. Justin said that the lightning, itself, seemed to become a shield around the car. Perhaps you merely coaxed it to act outside the circumstances it was created for. You bade it help you instead of harm you."

Elli sat for a moment, pondering what Marion had said until curiosity got the better of her. "What else can my powers do? Can I make an oak tree grow anywhere? Or make a ball of fire appear?"

"Yes and no. It all depends on the situation. To grow an oak tree or any plant, you need a seed to begin with or some fiber of the original. By searching deep in the soil, you can often find plants that have been hibernating. Fire and water are much the same. One rule will most ultimately pertain even to your astounding powers. You cannot create what is not already there."

"And air?"

"Air is perhaps the most easily found element but also the most fickle. Weather changes constantly, even when you don't feel it, and it is difficult to control. Storms tend to want to mount when you want just a slight rain. I won't mislead you, child. Each element has its good and bad points. It all depends on the side that you intend to nurture. The Acolytes and their apprentices delve into the almost uncontrollable side.

"Worse, they often combine their powers together, mixing them to enhance or even alter the natural order of things. For example, they can mix fire and water together, two natural enemies, and create dangerous things like fire rain. You would know it better as acid rain."

"But," Elli began, pondering the woman's words, "don't elements combine naturally on their own? Like how fire cannot burn without air?"

"It is true that the elements need each other in many ways, but at the same time they still can be each other's undoing. Water can put out fire, fire can melt earth, and so on. However, the Acolytes force the elements to perform unnaturally. To fight against nature, herself, while also embracing the chaotic side of magic makes their magic a greater risk, but it also increases their power as they let the elements get the better of them."

"Don't they worry about not being able to stop sometimes?"

"Ah, those who crave power often take little stock of the consequences as long as they attain their goal."

"There's something I've been meaning to ask you since

you told me about my powers of telepathy."

"Go on," Marion replied, crossing her hands in her lap.

"Could... Could the Acolytes have heard my thoughts like Justin and the others?" Elli asked, fearing the answer.

"It is probable that the answer is no. That is one of the more puzzling attributes about this form of telepathy. We cannot read the minds of our enemies any more than they can read ours. It is as if the balance that created us set up a wall between our minds. A blessing and a curse in many aspects as you can plainly see. Now, you should understand that the barrier is only established once you've chosen a side. If you delayed in deciding whether you would join the light or the dark, both sides would have had the chance to hear your thoughts."

Though Elli didn't like the sound of Marion's answer as she remembered how her thoughts had bounced between Justin and Derek those first two days, she sighed, knowing that there was nothing she could do about it now. All that was left was to press on. "How do I tap into the elements?"

"You have to find your center. Every elemental has one though each is unique. For myself, I tend to envision that I'm a tree, and I strip away layer upon layer of bark until I reach the inner seed where my power begins. Once you find your center, you will be able to call on the elements whenever you wish."

"My center? Okay, how do I go about finding it?"

"Close your eyes, child, and take deep breaths." Marion's voice was soothing, and it was easy to do as she asked. "Let yourself relax. Breathe deeply. In and out. In and out. Let yourself fall into the center of your magic. In and out. In and out...." As the old woman spoke, Elli felt herself begin to loosen up. The anxiety that had pervaded her mind since making the plan was finally ebbing away, leaving a kind of peaceful confidence in its wake. She let her mind drift where it will.

"In and out... in and out...."

It was so unlike her visions which tore through her mind on a rampage, leaving her senses painfully high-strung. Elli remembered different places she'd traveled with her parents. Smelled the warm spices of India. Tasted the sweetness of Georgia peaches. Heard the patter of English rain. *England... Clandestine...* Among the sensations of her past, Elli felt her mind pulled to a small room in a stone building and a blue, velvet box. Music that sounded like tinkling crystals in a breeze. *The tiara...* Elli saw the crown before her eyes. But it wasn't the music or the gold leaves spiraling around the coronet that caught her memory. Or the way the headpiece felt nestled in her hair. It was the cluster of five stones at the very center. A ruby... *fire.* An emerald... *earth.* Topaz... *air* Sapphire... *water.* Amethyst... *me. I've found it.*

"Yes, child, you have," Marion said though Elli wasn't sure if the woman had spoken in her mind or aloud. It didn't matter. The only thing that did was that she'd found her center.

***

Elli opened her eyes and stared at the mighty oak door before her. In her mind, she found the green emerald that contained her powers of earth, and inside it, a green flame burned, pulsing to be used. Pulling the power from the stone, she felt a sudden wave of overwhelming peace. Of normalcy. Of rightness. She'd been born to do this. Reaching out her hand, Elli spoke in her mind to the wooden door.

Let me in. Release, my friend. Let me pass.

Before her very eyes, Elli watched the oak come to life, stretching to allow her entry. Branches and leaves began to sprout and grow up the side walls, tendrils latching onto the old stone, twisting the heavy, rod-iron straps as if they were no more than paper. The magic felt wonderful in Elli's veins, making her want to laugh with delight. It was amazing to watch the door grow and spread until there was an opening.

Pulling her magic back into the emerald in her mind, Elli walked confidently through the passage entrance, and switched on the mini-flashlight that she'd stuck in her back pocket. The light played on the walls and into the ever-stretching blackness. With a silent thank-you to the oak tree that now sprouted from the aging rock of Clandestine, Elli ventured into the darkness, her confidence wavering at what she knew lay before her. Memories of a gangrene-colored blob invaded her mind, making cold sweat run down her back.

Branda. Think of Branda. The silence was heavy with only Elli's labored breathing and the occasional drip of water to break it. Her eyes were useless outside the small, yellow sphere of her light. Coming to a fork in the passage, she sighed heavily and glanced down at her watch. *Oh, perfect. I've been in here for half-an-hour and I have no idea which way to go? I never thought that I'd even get this far. Maybe Justin was wrong.*

"Welcome, Allison Wafe. We've been expecting you," a cold voice said from behind her, booming down the hall like thunder, filling her heart with dread.

Not even bothering to wonder how he got behind her, Elli barely had time to turn around and stare into his dark eyes before her light went out

***

"Ow! Teddy, you stepped on my foot," Page whispered, her voice loud to Justin's ears.

"Sorry." He sounded sheepish.

"*Shhh! Are you trying to get us killed?*" Justin replied, his telepathic message full of annoyance.

"*I hope no one heard,*" Cyn Dal added.

"*Sorry,*" Teddy and Page apologized in unison.

With a shake of his head, Justin focused his attention once more on where he was pointing the beam from his light. He hadn't liked dropping Elli off to let her fend for herself. The thought of Blackwell or the dean even *looking* at her made him want to grind his teeth. Elli should be back at Ravenwood, safe. He'd never thought of himself as the over-protective type and had even scorned that trait in others. But now? Now he understood.

That's why this screwball plan had irked him from the beginning. It all depended on a trap door that she'd seen during drama class. His argument that theaters tended to have trap doors in them had fallen on deaf ears. She'd convinced herself that she'd uncovered the entrance to a passageway in the floor that none of the blueprints even remotely mentioned. The closest thing to an entrance was a water pipe that came out from under the auditorium. It was pure, dumb luck that they'd only had to crawl a short way before it connected to a much larger tunnel.

"God, I hope this isn't a dead end," Justin thought, trying to quiet his thoughts.

"That makes two of us," Cyn Dal replied, moving her light over the ceiling of the tunnel, searching for any kind of hidden ladder leading up.

"Where did Elli say she saw the entrance?" Page asked, trying to keep her balance despite the small trickle of water that made the floor slippery, her backpack slung over one shoulder.

"She said it was somewhere in the make-up room. We should be right under it, I think," Teddy said, taking the light from Cyn Dal and holding it up higher to see.

"I hope Elli's all right," Page said. *"We've been searching for half-an-hour. What if we can't find it?"*

"We'll find it," Justin said, trying to hide how her words had made his stomach clench with worry. *Don't think about her*, he told himself, blocking his thoughts from the others. *Don't think about her or what might be happening to her right now. They need her alive. They can't hurt her... not yet.*

"Shut up!" he yelled, so distraught that he was unaware he'd sent the message through his telepathic link.

"Sorry, Justin. I didn't mean it," Page said, an apologetic frown on her pixie-like face.

"I was talking to myself," he admitted. *"I just can't...."*

"We know," Cyn Dal said, laying a hand on his shoulder. He could feel the chill in it even through his jacket. In reflex, he sent a wave of warmth into her through that light

connection, chasing the cold from his friend who smiled in response.

"*Let's just do this. The sooner we get the hell out of here, the better –*"

"*I found it!*" Teddy's voice rang loudly in their minds, cutting Justin off.

Patting Cyn Dal's hand, Justin quickly ran forward, his feet making a splashing sound in the hollow tunnel. He found Teddy standing under a hole in the ceiling, his light dancing up into oblivion. Justin could just barely see the last rung of a ladder a few feet up on the side wall.

"*How are we going to get the ladder down? It's even too high for me to reach,*" Teddy said.

"*I think I can get it down,*" Cyn Dal said, stepping out from behind Page. Justin watched her almond-shaped eyes close. Though he only felt a slight tremor through the telepathic connection between them, he knew that she was gathering her powers around her. When Cyn Dal opened her eyes, Justin wasn't surprised to see that they had changed from a dark brown color to a vibrant, shimmering blue. He watched as she raised a hand and pointed toward the water that flowed at their feet. With a flick of her wrist, a thin column rose from the stream, stretching up into the tunnel over their head. As Cyn Dal curled her fingers into a grip and let her arm fall to her side, the water seemed to mimic her, grasping the bottom rung of the ladder and pulling it down with a splash.

"*Great!*" Page exclaimed when Cyn Dal had let the water return to its natural position, receiving a humble smile in return.

"*Let's get out of here,*" Justin said, putting his weight on the first rung. "*Elli might already be in trouble.*" Once at the top of the ladder, he put out his hand to touch the ceiling, feeling around for some kind of catch but finding none. The surface was smooth and felt cold against his wet hand. "*I think we have a problem. I can't find any way to open it.*"

"*This has to be the one, though,*" Teddy argued. "*It's in the right place.*"

"*Anyone got any bright ideas?*" Justin asked, frustrated. In his mind, he could hear the tick of a clock. Time was running out.

"*Let me try,*" Page said from below him. Once again Justin felt the tremble in the link while Page centered herself. Glancing down, he saw her eyes turn to a golden yellow that always reminded him of owl eyes, and he felt a breeze blow past him as it tested the ceiling for cracks. "*This is the right place. I can see the make-up room over our heads. I'll try and open the hatch.*" The breezes seemed to strengthen around Justin, blowing through his hair and making his red, button-down shirt billow under his brown, leather jacket. There was a slight whistling sound through the tunnel.

"*Page. You have to keep the noise down. Someone might hear!*" Cyn Dal said, clutching the now-icy rungs of the ladder.

"*Don't worry. No one will notice since it's started to rain outside.*" Page's telepathic voice sounded hollow in Justin's mind, but he was too busy watching as the lid began to lift over his head.

"*Great job, Page,*" he sent back to her, letting her know she could stop as he put out his hand to keep it from banging as it blew open. Crawling through the opening, Justin let his torch flash around the room while he helped the others up. When they were all standing in a circle, he said, "*Okay. You all know what to do. We've only got one chance at this, so let's get it right.*"

"*Good luck to you, too,*" Page said, rolling her eyes at him as she headed toward the door.

Before Cyn Dal could follow, Teddy put a tender hand on her shoulder, stopping her. "Be safe," he whispered aloud in her ear. Justin turned his back to the couple just as Cyn Dal's small, pale hand covered Teddy's large, dark one, his chest tightening with bitter sweetness. Only when he heard the door close behind him did he turn back around.

"*Ready?*" Teddy asked.

"*As I'll ever be.*"

Chapter 4

Though no light shown from under the dean's office door, Page and Cyn Dal still crept silently down the hallway. It'd been easy getting this far, perhaps a little too easy; the halls had been dimly lit but empty. And though she didn't want to question their good luck, Cyn Dal had butterflies in her stomach.

"*You know, I'd like to know where all the students are,*" she said, slipping from shadow to shadow, Page at her heels.

"*Well, since the secret is out, maybe they all left,*" Page replied, clutching her backpack tightly with one hand, keeping her flashlight aimed at the floor.

"*I don't know about that. If you were a psychotic, power-hungry group of elementals, would you let them go? Don't you think you'd have some kind of plan to use them as hostages or zombie guards or something?*"

Page froze where she was, her gray eyes filled with horror. "*That's just way too creepy. Let's just get what we can and get out.*"

With a nod, Cyn Dal, in a crouch, crossed the remaining stretch of hall to the dean's office door. She could feel Page kneel behind her, watching her back, peering down the hallway for any sign of movement. Putting her eye to the key hole, her heart beating loudly, her throat dry, Cyn Dal gazed inside, crossing her fingers. *"It's empty,"* she said, twisting the doorknob, *"and locked. What do we do? Your magic would be too noisy, and we aren't exactly sitting in a puddle."*

"No worries!" Page exclaimed. *"I came prepared."* Swinging her backpack around, Page unzipped it and pulled out a small crowbar.

"And here I thought you were searching for some lockpicks," Cyn Dal said, surprised.

"Who do I look like? Nancy Drew?" Page retorted as she jammed the end of the crowbar between the door and the jam and began to pry it open.

As Cyn Dal waited, chills crept up her arms, making the shadows down the hall seem more threatening. *"Hurry, Page. I don't like sitting here in the open."*

"Nearly got it.... There!"

Cyn Dal heard an audible pop and the breaking of wood as the door flew open. Turning back, Cyn Dal watched as her friend disappeared through the door and then followed her, still shivering. It wasn't until she closed the heavy door behind them that she began to feel a little better. *"Let's make this quick,"* she said, switching on her flashlight.

The room was in the same shambles that it had been in when Page and Elli had visited it a week ago. Papers and books were strewn about the office, piled in every possible place. Though there was some benefit to it as no one would ever be able to guess what they'd looked through, it also left them at a loss as to where to begin.

"I can't see much reason in taking these books. They can't be very valuable the way he's thrown them around," Page said, waving her flashlight around the room until it came to rest on the mahogany cabinet behind the desk. *"I guess I'll try opening that if you want to look through the desk. Elli said something about a notebook that the dean was writing in. Maybe we'll get lucky."*

"Okay," Cyn Dal replied, trying to hide the way her hands were shaking. This just didn't feel right. It was like something

was bearing down on them. Gritting her teeth and telling herself it was just nerves, she picked her way across the mine field of items that lay haphazardly on the maroon carpeting. After all, they were in the middle of the Acolytes' territory. It was little wonder that she felt jumpy. Cyn Dal began to leaf through the items on the dean's desk, finding mostly papers and file folders full of administrative information. Pulling out the drawers was almost as fruitless. *"Having any luck?"* she asked while still digging around.

"I'm working on it," Page replied. Cyn Dal could hear the sound of plastic scraping metal as her friend tried to open the cabinet like she had the office door.

"Keep trying," she said, reaching out her hand for the last drawer in the desk to find it jammed with legal pads and other office material. *"The desk is a waste. There isn't anything in it but loose paper clips."*

"Try looking around the bookshelves. Maybe you'll find something they overlooked."

Shrugging, Cyn Dal made her way over to the bookcase next to the bathroom, reading the titles that lay at odd angles on the shelves. Not sure if it would do any good, she began to pull them out, examining their bindings and reveling in their old-book smell.

"Hey! I got it!" Page said from behind her. Turning excitedly, nearly knocking over a pile of papers, Cyn Dal found the red-head opening the mahogany door and peering inside, the reflection of her flashlight leaving strange shadows on the wall. *"Wait a minute! This can't be right!"* Page's exasperated tone made Cyn Dal rush to her side.

"What's wrong?"

"It's empty. Where are the scrolls and things that Elli said she saw in here?" her voice sounding annoyed.

Glancing inside, Cyn Dal found that the cabinet was indeed bare. Not even dust marred the glossy finish of the mahogany. *"Why would they lock up an empty cabinet?"* she wondered, more to herself than Page, her curiosity peeked. *"It seems like such a ridiculous thing to do... unless it really isn't* empty!"

"*Am I blind? Do you see anything in here 'cause I sure don't?*" Page exclaimed, waving her hands around inside, meeting no resistance.

"*What if it's a trick? Maybe the back slides open or something. Try looking around for some kind of trigger.*"

Making their way around the room, Cyn Dal and Page moved the books on the shelves, trying to find some kind of catch, but, to their great disappointment, discovering nothing. They shifted the papers on the floor looking for a switch, it proving to be an even greater waste of time.

Moving to the window, Cyn Dal began to dig through the books under the sill, finding nothing. Desperate and unsure of where else to look, she sat back on her heels, pushing a strand of hair that had escaped her braid from her face. It was then that she saw something strange about the sill itself, or more precisely, the stone beneath it. Running her finger along the masonry, she found that it had been worn smooth by something. Curious, she leaned in, trying to get her light in the right position to see, but finding nothing.

Shaking her hand, Cyn Dal put her hands on the sill, pushed herself up, and was surprised to feel it give under her weight. Pushing harder, she found that it slid further down and stopped with a sudden click followed by the sound of wood sliding on wood.

"*Page, I found it!*" she cried in her mind, hurrying to the open cabinet, Page behind her. It appeared, to their amazement, that the ceiling inside had come down like a dumb waiter, bringing with it a treasure-trove of different things, one being a large book carved with archaic symbols. Picking it up, Cyn Dal found that the cover was made of wood and felt very familiar in her hands. Unable to speak, she simply held it in her hands in disbelief.

"*Cyn Dal, is that what I think it is?*" Page asked, her telepathic voice sounding almost squeaky.

"*I think so,*" she replied in amazement.

"*Merlin's second book,*" they said in unison, looking at

each other and then back to the volume in wonder.

"We've found it! Our kind has been looking for it for hundreds of years and here it is! In our hands!" Page's exclamations made Cyn Dal shake with adrenaline.

"We have to get it out of here," she said shakily, clutching it to her chest protectively, like it would fall into dust in her hands.

Looking back toward the cabinet, Page added with excitement, *"There's more!"* A leather-bound notebook lay under where the volume had lain. But even more important than the journal was a small case made of some black material, about the size of a hard-cover book.

"This is it!" Page whispered, shinning her flashlight down on the box which seemed to shimmer with a strange kind of pearl-like luster. *"This must be the box from Elli's vision."* In awe, she reverently picked it up and placed it, along with the notebook, in her bag. *"I can't believe we have it all. The box, Dean Clandestine's journal, and Merlin's second book."*

With Merlin's book still clutched in her hands, not ready to press their luck any further, Cyn Dal whispered, *"Let's go."*

"I don't think so," a hard voice said as the room flooded with light, freezing Page and Cyn Dal before they could walk away from the cabinet.

Blinking in the glare, Cyn Dal's eyes focused on who had entered the room and her blood turned to ice water....

***

"You know, I've always hated chemistry," Justin said, his light playing on the chemistry lab door. *"I despise memorizing the table of elements. It seems like such a waste of time."*

Realizing that his friend was just making small talk so he wouldn't have to think about Elli, Teddy said nothing, not wanting to increase his friend's unease. There had been no problems reaching the chemistry department on the second floor of Clandestine. All the hallways had been empty.

"So, why don't we knock on the door and see if anyone's

home," Justin added, his telepathic voice dripping with sarcasm.

Reaching out his hand, Teddy let it rest on the handle, breathing deeply before opening the door. It was unlikely that anyone would be in the chemistry lab this time of night and there was no light shining through the frosted glass window of the door, but something just didn't sit right with him. There was this nagging feeling in the pit of his stomach.

"*What's wrong? What are you waiting for?*" Justin asked, impatiently.

"*I don't know. Nothing I guess,*" Teddy replied, feeling the tips of his ears warm with anxiety. Turning the brass handle, the door swung easily open on well-greased hinges, and they quickly went inside and closed it behind them. The metallic faucets of the sinks flashed in the light as Teddy and Justin looked around; the room had a lingering smell of anti-bacterial soap and old chemicals. Long, black counters with small, silver nozzles sticking out of them were set in rows with an occasional loose beaker setting around on the granite tabletops.

"*You know,*" Justin began, walking over to a gas spout, "*I think it's high time that this place was remodeled.*"

"*How are we going to do this? We have to have at least some time before setting it off. It isn't like we can just light a match, turn on the gas, and run away.*"

"*I guess all those years of watching television are about to pay off.*" Justin's voice was almost reckless as he turned the nozzle to the "on" position. The strong smell of gas began to pour from the silver spout. "*I've already got the bang part figured out,*" he added, pulling a lighter from his pocket, the gold plating flashing in the glow from his flashlight. "*Help me turn on all the gas lines.*"

As they made their way around the room, the itch that something was wrong began to grow to an all-consuming worry. A knot formed in his stomach, almost as if an invisible fist were clenching and unclenching his insides. Teddy tried to wave the feeling away as a reaction to the gas that was quickly filling the room. He walked to the last table that sat by the windows and reached for the last silver nozzle.

"Ready for demolition?" Justin asked, coming up behind him.

Before Teddy could answer, there was a loud bang and the sound of cracking glass behind them as the room flooded with light. Jerking around, they saw a blue-haired boy standing with his arms crossed, leaning against the inside of the door frame, his lanky shadow playing on the wall behind him.

"Hi, Arnie," Justin said, his voice bitter. "What brings you to the chemistry lab? More hair dye?"

"Funny, Spaller. You won't think it's so funny when the dean gouges your eyes out so you can watch yourself die." The relaxed cockiness that Arnie was displaying made Teddy wary.

"*Justin*," he said telepathically, "*something isn't right here. There's no way Arnie could take us both down. He's half my size at least.*"

Justin agreed silently with Teddy's suspicions. Aloud he said, "So, Arnie, why don't you just get out of the way and we'll leave?"

"I've got a better idea," he said, smelling the air. "You two shut off the gas valves and come with me. You don't want to miss the show after all."

"What show?" Teddy asked, his eyes looking past Arnie to the hall as a tall figure appeared. "*I think his back up has arrived.*" Teddy watched as a thin but muscular hand shoved Arnie out of the way so its owner could enter. Now standing just inside the room was the beady-eyed history teacher, Mr. Yarrow, whose long nose sniffed at the gas that was rapidly filling the chemistry lab, his action reminding Teddy of a rat sniffing cheese.

"Ah, Mr. Spaller and Mr. Korran. Baking?" The teacher's monotone voice was laced with danger. "It seems you've left the burners on." Teddy felt a sudden wind blow by him and a flash of silver caught his eye as all the gas nozzles turned off. "Ah, much better. The room should clear in a moment."

A smug smile crept over Arnie's face as he saw their enemy's plan defeated.

"Now," Mr. Yarrow continued, crossing his arms over his black-robed chest, "I believe Mr. Klimet offered you seats for our little experiment tonight."

"What are you talking about?" Justin's voice sounded hard to Teddy's ears.

"Why the binding of Miss Wafe's powers, of course. It's really a rather simple operation though it does have some nasty side effects. Think of losing a limb but going through the pain of the severing until the power is released again. I've seen elementals driven mad with it. But there's no help for it, I'm afraid. We can't very well keep her contained if she's able to use her –"

Through Mr. Yarrow's speech, Teddy had felt a tension building through his telepathic link with Justin and the sudden release of it was like a small bomb that rippled through the web. Before Teddy could even react, Justin charged at the sadistic pedagogue, his fists clenched and a madness in his eyes. In the millisecond it took to watch Yarrow's hands fly up and Arnie ready himself to spring forward and protect one of his masters, Teddy felt a drawing-in around him. He saw his friend slam into an invisible wall made from the air in the chemistry lab. Justin was thrown backwards and lay sprawled on the floor.

Helping Justin to his feet, feeling himself flush with anger, an emotion he rarely felt, Teddy stepped to the air wall and pounded with all his strength only to watch the wall wave and bend as if it were made of plastic wrap, but not break. Looking through the force field, Teddy watched Mr. Yarrow cross his arms and shake his head.

"You shouldn't interrupt your elders, young man," the pedagogue said.

Out of the corner of his eye, Teddy saw Justin approach the wall. The madness was gone from his eyes, but his features emanated danger.

"I was just about to thank you for bringing her to us," Mr.

Yarrow continued. "We probably couldn't have done it without you. Of course, the rest of you are just a bonus. I'm looking forward to teaching you the correct use of pain. Miss Aster is a slow learner, but I have high hopes for you two gentlemen and the young ladies who are, at this very moment, being taken care of by my colleague. You see my friends, you have lost the war even before the battle has begun."

Leaning his head against the spongy air wall, Teddy tried to ignore the desperation that was settling over his shoulders. He could hear Justin's struggles to get through the barrier and his friend's loud cursing at their enemies, but his mind was reeling, trying to find an escape but unable to. Breathing deeply, he had to squelch a sneeze as he inhaled the powerful scent of gas. Teddy could feel his muscles tighten as a plan erupted in his brain. Without looking at Justin so as not to give himself away, he concentrated hard on the image of his friend in his mind. *"The wall is made of gas. The old lunatic concentrated it for us!"*

Justin backed away from the barrier and angrily shoved his hands in his pockets. "You know what, Yarrow," he said as Teddy came to stand beside him. "I think you've really underestimated my friends and I."

"Have I?" The teacher raised an eyebrow as his beady, yellow eyes darkened. "What makes you so confident, young man?"

"Just two simple things. The first is that we would all rather walk through hell before we'd let you win this war. In fact, you'll never win as long as at least one of us still breathes." Justin let his eyes drop to the floor as if he was studying it and crossed his arms over his chest.

"And the second?" Mr. Yarrow's voice was smug as he walked toward the wall, stopping a foot from the barrier.

When Justin looked up to match gazes with the gangly professor, Teddy saw that his friend's eyes appeared as if they were made of flame. "I've got a lighter." Before the teacher could react, Justin flipped open the lid, ran the striker down his leg and threw the small flame at the gas saturated wall. As

Teddy threw up his arms to protect his face, he barely had time to send a signal to the others through their telepathic web as a terrible rumble nearly knocked him off his feet. He could hear windows popping from the white-hot heat, the screaming of timbers and the roar of flames in his ears. Letting his arms slowly fall, he saw that Justin had formed a protective ring around them both, keeping them from the explosion. It was almost as if they were inside a glass tube. The flames roared above them and to all sides, but Teddy couldn't smell any smoke or feel the heat from the inferno. Sight and sound were the only evidence of the fire around them.

"The roof's gone!" Justin yelled, sweat from the exertion of holding back the flames running down his face. "The fire is feeding on the air now that the gas has burned off! We've got to get out of here! I can't hold it back much longer!"

"We can't go out the window! We're on the second floor! Can you keep the barrier up so we can get to the door?" Teddy heard his voice almost drowned out by the noise.

"I think so!" He felt a tremor in the web as Justin squeezed his eyes shut and concentrated. A fiery tunnel appeared before them, leading to the door and smoke-filled hallway. They followed it, feeling the flames close in behind them with every step, and stumbled through the door.

With his back to the hallway, Justin stood in the door frame of the fiery lab. Teddy could feel his focus on the inferno and could sense, through Justin, the fire's powerful desire to consume the rest of the school. All it had to do was get past the small door frame.

Afraid to break his friend's concentration, Teddy watched as Justin reached his hand back inside the lab and grabbed a large fistful of fire. Justin proceeded to twist that handful of fire, grabbing more as he needed to from the inferno, until it was nothing but a long, braided coil of fire in his hand of about a two-inch thickness. He then laced it back and forth across the doorway, creating a back burn that would not allow the fire access to the hallway. The entire process took only a matter of minutes.

"It won't last long," Justin said, turning back around.

It was then that they both noticed the body lying at their feet. It was Arnie. He was unconscious and his hair was damp with blood from where his head had smacked the wall when he had been thrown backward. His clothes were still smoking, and through the charred remains of his shirt sleeves, they could see burnt flesh. It appeared like he had thrown up his hands to protect his face and had burned both his arms and hands terribly.

"We can't leave him here! He'll die!" Teddy said as he began to lift Arnie.

"It's no more than he'd do for us," Justin snapped, whipping sweat from his face.

Pinning Justin with a look of annoyance that he rarely used, Teddy replied sharply, "We're supposed to be the good guys, remember? I have no problem defeating someone in a fair fight, but I won't leave him here to burn alive if the fire leaks through your net."

Teddy could feel his friend's conflicted emotions, but in the end, Justin bent to help him. Together, they carried the unconscious boy down the stairs and laid him down gently on the floor, safely away from the blaze in the lab.

"Did you see where Yarrow went?" Teddy asked, leaning against the wall for a brief rest.

"No. Once I tossed the fireball from my lighter, I had to act quickly, or we would've been roasted. I don't know if he made it out or not." Running his hand through his hair, he added, "But it doesn't matter. We have to go. If it's true that Elli has been captured, we have to find her before the dean can bind her magic." Without another word between them, they began to run down the hall toward the old wing.

Chapter 5

The precious cargo in her backpack felt heavy in her hands under Ms. Bellstone's liquid, glinting eyes, but Page refused to let it drop. She stood, stubborn and unyielding, her back to the window, Cyn Dal beside her, while the woman in the black robe entered the dean's office, Cami Valance in skin-tight leather following.

"Well, my girls, what is it you have there?" Ms. Bellstone asked, her nasal voice sarcastic.

"I'm impressed. I didn't know you goodie-goods would stoop to stealing," Cami added, her bright red finger nails gesturing at the book Cyn Dal clutched.

"Shut up, you slut!" Page snarled, glaring at the other girl. Cami looked as though she were about to hiss in response but stopped when Ms. Bellstone held up her hand.

"Let's be civil about this. After all, we exist in a symbiotic relationship and in respect to that, I want you two young ladies to hand over the items you've stolen and come with us." Ms. Bellstone crossed her pudgy arms, her wrist watch – the band covered in large, gaudy fish with sparkling tails – flashing in the light.

"I don't think so," Page said, swinging her backpack up to rest squarely on her back. The politeness in Ms. Bellstone's voice made her skin crawl. *"Got any bright ideas?"* she asked Cyn Dal silently.

"The window is our only option. We're not getting out

the same way we came in, that's for sure, unless you have some other magical remedy in your pack."

"Oh, you're so funny," she retorted. *"I'm glad you've still got a sense of humor under the circumstances."*

"Tsk, tsk, ladies. It's rude to talk amongst yourselves when others are in the room," Ms. Bellstone interjected. Though she couldn't hear what Page and Cyn Dal were saying, it was obvious they were speaking telepathically. "Now, I won't ask again. Give us Merlin's things or I'll have to resort to drastic measures."

"Why isn't she just whisking them away? Or better yet, why isn't she ordering Cami to do it since she has the power of air?" Page asked. *"Water might not be useful since it isn't exactly raining in here, but air should be no problem."*

"I don't know. Maybe they can't be taken by force or maybe they're beyond elemental magic."

"Girls," Ms. Bellstone's voice rang loudly in the narrow space of the dean's office. "I'm waiting."

"Oh, let me try, Ms. Bellstone," Cami whined. "I think I can suck the air from around them. When their faces are blue, maybe they'll feel more like cooperating."

"Very well." The teacher looked at her pupil with appreciation and pride.

Page could feel alarm in the air as she watched Cami's violet eyes turn dark and become gold-flecked. She felt a kind of pulling and sensed, rather than saw, the vacuum which was about to encompass them. Quickly grasping at her own powers of air in retaliation, she pushed back at the wave of air magic that would have consumed both Cyn Dal and herself, leaving them breathless. She watched as Cami's eyes narrowed, feeling the pressure increase and the weight of the malice behind it strengthening.

Though all of her concentration was on the leather-clad girl, Page noticed a sardonic smile creep over Ms. Bellstone's face as the older woman raised her hand and rested it on Cami's shoulder, adding her power to the girl's. It was then that the suffocating weight became too much for Page. Gritting her teeth, her muscles tense, she barely felt Cyn Dal take her hand to add her strength to the fight. It was as if she had been given a glass of water after a desert crossing. The force pressing down on her was still strong and heavy, but Cyn Dal's presence took the edge off. Page knew, however, that they both couldn't last long with a full powered Acolyte and one of the Dark Army bearing down of them with such power.

"*Cyn Dal,*" she gasped, her mental voice shaky even to her. "*You have to let go. You have to break the window and get out. Take Merlin's history and box to Elli.*"

"*No! We're not losing you, too! You can't hold them off by yourself. You'll be destroyed!*" Cyn Dal sounded frantic at even the idea of leaving Page behind.

"*Well, I'm up for any other ideas,*" she replied, almost buckling as a wave of pain crashed over her, like a million pins being stuck in her brain in rapid succession.

"*It's raining outside!*" Cyn Dal exclaimed. "*Can you hold them for a moment?*"

"*Hurry!*" As soon as Cyn Dal released her hand, Page felt the full weight of all that evil bearing down her. Closing her eyes, she took every last ounce of strength she had and pushed back. The room was growing warmer by the second as the air molecules rubbed against each other, unsure of whose command to follow. The smell of ozone filled her nostrils as the crystal sound of breaking glass rang out behind her. Wind-blown rain showered down on her, tightening her mop of red hair into ringlets.

Through the noise and pressure in her tired mind, Page heard the blessed sound of Teddy's voice yelling a warning. "*Head's up!*" An explosion rang out in the distance, the vibration of it bringing Page, Cami and Ms. Bellstone to their knees and gratefully releasing Page from the battle of wills. Opening her watery eyes, she saw that Ms. Bellstone and Cami were slowly pulling themselves to their feet. Fear gripped her insides as she realized that she didn't have the strength to fight them anymore. Prepared for the end, Page watched a wave of water crash down on her enemies from behind her, shoving the dark Acolyte and her companion out the door and slamming it. The water then broke into two separate columns, one going to the door and spreading itself thin so no one could enter the dean's office, the other moving towards her and lifting her from the carpeting to carry her outside the window to where Cyn Dal waited.

"Thanks," she said, her real voice sounding squeaky to her ears, the rain cooling her flushed cheeks. Giving her a smile, Cyn Dal let the column shorten and bring Page to stand on her own two rubbery legs, the pack still slung across the red-head's back. Taking her friend's limp arm, Cyn Dal rested it across her shoulders and helped her friend down the hill toward the van, one arm around Page's waist and the other still clinging to Merlin's precious book.

***

The blindfold felt scratchy on her eyelids, but Elli didn't dare try to lift her hands to remove it or the overly-muscular ox, Ash Quillet, who drug her along by her increasingly bruised left arm, would squeeze harder. She had to rely on other sensations besides sight to help her out of this. The dean had personally seen to her capture in the passageway. *I suppose I should feel flattered*, she thought, listening to the sound of both her and her captors' feet echoing off stone walls. They must have left the dark and gloomy passage behind as the dank smell no longer filled her nose. Instead, the smell of burning torches, the rustle of the dean's robe, and the clink of chains tickled her senses, making her wonder where she was being led. She had lost all sense of direction.

After several more minutes, Elli felt herself enter a room. She could hear the crackling of a large fire and the popping of wood echoing off high ceilings, as she was forced into a chair and the blind fold removed. After glaring at Ash who now stood off to her side, Elli rubbed her sore arm as she looked around, searching for a way to escape. She was in what must have been a small oratory when the building was still used by the church. Torches lined the walls while candles had been shoved in every niche available. Though it had long since been removed, the outline of a large cross could still be seen on the stones of one wall.

A large fire burned in a concave dish which was set on four stone legs, just to the left of where Elli sat. Pews, which had seen better days, were shoved haphazardly against the walls. Some of them had wax congealed on their once-polished surfaces, while others were heavily scratched, missing large chunks of wood, or appeared to have been scorched. The dish on the raised dais had probably been used for private baptisms at one time. Elli couldn't help but feel the irony in how something that had once been used for a holy ceremony was now a firepit used by the Acolytes.

It only took her a moment to take all of this in before her heart sank. It seemed that the only way out was the way they'd come in... and Dean Clandestine was between her and it.

"Welcome to the Room of Binding."

"Where's Branda?" she asked trying to ignore the way the sound of the word 'binding' made her shudder.

"Waiting for you to make the right choice," the dean explained, as if it was the simplest thing in the world.

"What are you talking about?"

"Oh, Miss Wafe." Dean Clandestine shook his head disappointedly, the motion making Elli's stomach sink. "Haven't you figured it out yet? You've been brought to this place to choose what is more important. The life of your friends or your own free will."

"You mean I have to choose between binding myself to you or Branda will...." She couldn't bring herself to say the last word.

"Not just Branda, my dear. You see, my colleagues and I knew you would be coming back for that ridiculous girl," Dean Clandestine said, smug in his malice.

"You were waiting for us." Elli's voice sounded hollow to her own ears. The room began to spin, and her little fingers tingled. *"Not now!"* she yelled at the premonition that was threatening to invade her mind. The last thing she needed was to lose consciousness and leave herself helpless. Concentrating on the dean, Elli was able to fight the vertigo. "Where's Branda?" she asked again, raising her voice, using her anger. "I want to see her now!"

"Patience, my dear. You'll see her presently. You –"

"Now!" Elli knew it was stupid to agitate the dean, but the fear-soaked rage that was gnawing at her insides made her careless. The dean paused for a moment, a variety of emotions playing on his face, all showing his fight for control over his temper - a fight he was losing.

However, the entrance of a handsome, dark-haired boy drew the dean's attention, staying his hand. As he approached, Elli's heart quickened as a memory flashed in her mind. A dark passageway. Derek Blackwell's haunted, brown eyes. His aid in her escape.

But that was then and this was now, something that was very plain to Elli when she looked into his eyes again. In them she only saw the same arrogance she'd seen on the day they'd first met. His every move seemed guarded as he neared the dean's side. He'd helped her once before, but would he again?

"Lady Allison," he said, stopping just short of where she was seated, his voice emotionless. As she started to rise, Elli felt Ash's heavy hands pressing her roughly back down. A flash of anger crossed Derek's eyes so quickly that she wasn't even sure it had been there; the only evidence of its existence was the quick removal of Ash's hands.

Leaning in close to the dean, Derek whispered something into his ear. A small smile crossed Dean Clandestine's lips as he whispered an order back to Derek who, without so much as another glance at Elli, left the room.

"It seems that my colleagues have anticipated your request, my dear," the dean said, a wicked gleam in his eye. With a gesture towards the door, the dean moved to the side.

As Elli stared, Derek returned with both Mr. Pelt and Mr. Drailinger at his side. Behind them followed two others that Elli didn't know. The trailing two carried someone between them. As they approached her, Elli had to fight the reflex to recoil. The two boys walking toward her had no irises in their eyes - only whites, like deep-sea fish. And yet, though their faces had no emotion, Elli had the shocking realization that she knew the people starring back at her. *Oh, my God! You're from my history class!* She flashed back to the faces that had stared at her the day Mr. Yarrow had taken Branda and herself to the dean.

"What did you do to them?" she gasped.

"It's a mere control spell. It's amazing what you can do with a person's mind when you control the water that surrounds it," Mr. Pelt said as he circled Elli's chair and knelt at her side, his hands clutching the arm, the jagged, chewed nails digging into the soft wood. His breath was hot and repugnant as he leaned in.

"And if you don't cooperate, we'll use it on you, too," Mr. Drailinger said, his blue eyes looking as they'd sunken into his bone-colored face. In the flickering light from the many torches and candles, he looked so much like a talking skull that it made Elli shiver.

"Now, that's no way to treat our guest," the dean chastised, his voice ringing with a self-satisfied air. With a grunt, Mr. Pelt stood and both he and Mr. Drailinger backed away from Elli's chair to stand several feet away. Mr. Pelt's thick lips spread in a smile, making his round face resemble a grinning jack-o-lantern.

The carriers dropped the person they were dragging in a heap at Elli's feet and then retreated out the door. Dropping to her knees beside the still girl, Elli rolled her over, a groan escaping the girl's lips.

"Branda," Elli whispered, holding her friend.

"What's left of her," Branda gasped. Her face was still strikingly beautiful despite the many cuts and abrasions that marked it. Her bottom lip was split and swollen, and her right eye could barely open due to how black it was. Her clothing was in rags, and her arms were cut, dried blood caking the wounds. Bruises peppered her white skin, though they had no effect on the large tattoo of an intertwined dragon and phoenix that ran from her left forearm, up her shoulder where it stopped just under her left eye. Kneeling on the cold stone floor beside her friend, Elli had to fight back tears as she cradled the brave girl.

"A lesson well taught, I see," the dean chortled.

At the dean's glee over Branda's torture, Elli felt an anger in her that she had never experienced before. Out of instinct, pain, and guilt, she unleashed her power on the fire that crackled beside her, calling it to strike at her enemies. Through the angry tears in her eyes, Elli watched the dark leaders of the Acolytes throw their arms up and the ball of fire glance off to extinguish in a puff of smoke.

"Very good. You have more power than I expected for an amateur," the dean said, smiling in delight. "You'll be magnificent once you've been trained."

Glaring at the dean, Elli reached again for her power, grabbing for an even larger amount, but was stopped by a mental groan.

"*There's no point. Save your strength for a battle you can win,*" Branda said, visibly wincing a little. Reluctantly Elli let her power ebb away as she helped her friend sit up.

"May we get on with it?" Mr. Pelt began. "It's time for you to take your place amongst our ranks. It's either that or all that you love will die. What this one has been through will be a Sunday stroll in the park compared to the suffering we'll inflict on others." When she refused to answer, Mr. Pelt hurried forward, grabbed her hair, and yanked her head back, forcing her to meet his gaze.

The premonition screamed through Elli's mind so quickly that she barely heard Derek's curse or Branda's weak yell of alarm. She could smell Mr. Pelt's breathe on her face and feel the pain in her scalp, but in a heartbeat, she was beyond it all.

Page and Cyn Dal facing Ms. Bellstone and Cami. Justin reaching for a lighter. Teddy yelling. A swirl of heat. Derek looking intensely into her eyes. The dean holding a sheet of paper with very familiar writing on it....

When the visions subsided, she found a standoff before her. She still knelt beside Branda who was now covered in sweat from some exertion, her eyes slowly turning from red to blue as she glared at Mr. Pelt who was nursing a burn on his hand. Derek was now nose-to-nose with an angry Ash as he stood between him and Elli and Branda. Mr. Pelt's face was set in a snarl as he stared at her from behind Ash. Both the dean and Mr. Drailinger had remained where they had stood, their expressions unreadable.

"Don't ever touch her again or Branda's burn will feel like a tickle in comparison to me," Derek growled, his voice filled with such poison that Elli flinched.

Elli silently asked Branda, *"Can you walk?"*

"Anything to get the hell out of here," she replied, slowly standing on her unsteady legs; all the while, Elli's attention was split between Branda and the standoff between Ash, Mr. Pelt, and Derek.

"Ha! It appears, dear colleagues, that this girl has worked her wiles on our Derek. Your weakness over her will be your undoing, boy," Mr. Pelt said, spittle spraying from his lips.

"The dean wants her undamaged for the ceremony," Derek threw back, his shoulders rigid with anger, "and the only undoing will be your own if you try that again."

"Try it," Ash said quietly, his eyes flashing dangerously. Whatever fear he'd felt toward Derek before seemed to have evaporated.

"Enough!" Dean Clandestine shouted, making Elli's heart jump. The three slowly backed down, though Ash and Derek continued to glare at each other. "What did you see, girl?" Dean Clandestine asked.

When he received nothing but icy coldness, his face darkened with impatience. "What did you see?" the dean yelled again.

When she still refused to answer, Mr. Drailinger sneered. "I wonder, Dean Clandestine, if it could be another poetic line. A message from one of the descendants of Merlin. 'How with this rage shall beauty hold a plea,'" he quoted, the words freezing Elli's blood. Her heart was beating loudly in her ears and the world seemed to dip and spin around her. The look on her face was confirmation enough for the Acolytes.

The dean took several steps forward, Mr. Drailinger keeping time with his steps as they approached. "Yes, we know about the lines. Allow me to alleviate the questions that I know are running through that pretty head of yours."

Reaching into the folds of his robe, the dean produced a piece of paper. He stepped closer towards them and Elli instinctively put Branda behind her. Holding his hand in the air as if he was offering an olive branch, he placed the paper in her hands, the action so much like her premonition that chills swept up her arms. At first glance, the sheet seemed blank. It was only when Elli moved it around in the firelight that she noticed impressions covering the paper from top to bottom. Her eyes widened and her stomach clenched when she recognized her own handwriting. Elli's mind traveled back to a scene in history class from several days before. A sheet of paper covered in scribbles and premonition predictions. Tearing it from her notebook to hand it to a demanding Mr. Yarrow. An extra sheet fluttering to the ground beside her desk, lying there forgotten in the excitement of Branda's ripping her notes from the teacher's hands and flinging them out the window.

Coming back to the present, Elli found the dean glaring at Branda who stood just behind Elli. "You stupid girl. You destroyed the original but in your adolescent arrogance you didn't think that there might be an impression made on the second page."

"I guess my consolation is that you don't know everything." Branda, though shaking from her wounds and use of her power against Mr. Pelt, was still as daring as ever.

"Not for long," he replied. In a matter of seconds, several things happened at once. The dean snapped his fingers and Branda yelled in alarm as Ash and Mr. Pelt grabbed her. Before Elli could even reach for her powers, Derek was pinning her arms behind her back, his breath hot on her neck as she struggled against him.

She stopped only when Mr. Drailinger pulled an ancient and extremely sharp looking dagger from his robe and handed it to the dean who placed it against Branda's neck. "Reach for your powers, Miss Wafe, and I'll cut her throat right in front of your eyes," Dean Clandestine said, his tone matter-of-fact. "I want to know the rest of the premonition and I want to know now."

"Don't tell him anything," Branda shouted.

"Silence!" the dean exclaimed, pressing the knife blade even closer to Branda's skin.

"Elli, tell him," Derek said, his voice sounding hallow to Elli's ears.

"No!" Branda cried. "They can't know. They'll be able to win!"

"Silence!" the dean roared. Elli watched as the blade nicked Branda's skin and a small trickle of blood began to run down her collar bone.

Elli felt Derek tense behind her. "You have to tell him. Do you think he'll bloody stop at just killing Branda? He'll hurt you, too!" he stressed. His voice almost sounded like he was begging, something the Acolytes also picked up on.

"See what I mean, Dean. The boy has gone soft over the girl," Mr. Pelt said, smugly.

"Maybe he'll have more of a stomach for blood when it's hers he's drinking," Ash added.

Elli felt Derek go very still behind her, though the tension in his body was like a lit cannon fuse, just waiting to go off. "Or maybe yours," he spat back in a very low, dangerous voice, his anger palpable.

The dean snarled, his eyes never leaving Elli's, "Enough! This is your last chance to save your friend, girl. Tell me what the lines mean."

"*Heads up!*" A split second after Teddy's call, Elli felt the floor pitch and heard an explosion echo through the high ceilings, knocking Mr. Drailinger into the dean who fell to the ground, the knife still clutched in his hands, and unsettling Mr. Pelt and Ash enough that Branda was able to twist away from them. Yelling at her to run, Derek suddenly pushed Elli behind him before tackling Ash and knocking him backward into the pews. Elli heard a crack as Ash's head connected with stone, dropping him.

"Get her!" the dean exclaimed, getting to his feet as the two blank-eyed students rushed back into the room at their master's command. Knowing she only had a few seconds, with her mind she reached for the charred, still-flaming wood in the fire, creating small shards of it that she quickly flung like a hail of bullets at her enemies. Mr. Pelt, Mr. Drailinger and the dean took cover, but even though the rain of flaming charcoal bits was hitting its targets, leaving welts, the students still charged forward. Mr. Drailinger reached into the pocket of his robe and pulled out a container of water. From it, he created a shield that made most of the fiery hail bounce away from the Acolytes and the blank-eyed students.

Getting to his feet, Derek grabbed her hand and they rushed through the door, Branda at their heels. In one deft movement, he called a fireball to him from one of the torches, slammed the door shut behind them, and then melted the metal latch to seal it shut.

"It won't hold them for long! Run," Derek yelled, throwing Branda's arm over his shoulder to help her.

As dust rained down from above, they hurried down the dimly lit hallway, Branda half running, half struggling to keep up. After several moments of blind panic, they came to a crossroads.

"Which way?" Branda asked, breathing heavily from the exertion of running on her pained legs and wiping sweat on her ragged sleeve.

"This way!" Derek said. "It'll be faster to head to the main door."

"Shhh!" Elli hissed, stopping in mid-step. Suddenly, the little hairs on the back of her neck began to raise and the adrenaline that had kept her going settled, making her muscles atrophy.

"What's wrong?" Derek asked.

"I thought I heard footsteps."

"Perfect. Just what we need!" Branda exclaimed, frustrated. "Try finding out who it is. Use the air to get a sense of who's coming and how quickly. You won't be able to see them since air can't take shape like other elements, but it should give you an idea."

Closing her eyes, Elli searched for the blazing yellow topaz in her mind at the same time she reached for a small breath of air. She let her spy roam through the halls where it brought back scents and the sound of footsteps nearing. There was a smell of burning apple wood and pine smoke. The sensation of lightning and the feel of soft leaves on her palm. It was then she knew.

"It's Justin!" she cheered, relief filling her. "He and Teddy are heading right for us. If we continue on, we'll run right into them."

"Thank, God! I thought it was the Acolytes. I'm not exactly in top fighting form, here," Branda said.

Excitement replacing the fear, Elli began to once again move down the hall, Derek and Branda at her side. Her green eyes peered through the dimly lit passage as she searched the shadows ahead. It was only a matter of moments before she saw two shapes rushing towards her from the gloom. Feeling her heart beat quicken, Elli smiled and nearly flew the last few steps down the hall, her anxiety suppressed by the thought of being in Justin's arms.

It took only a second to realize her mistake.

Seeing Derek rushing up behind her, both Justin and Teddy's eyes changed in an instant as they reached for their powers. "Elli, look out!" Justin yelled.

"No!" she screamed when she saw what they meant to do. She threw herself in front of Derek who was still holding the struggling Branda up.

"Get out of the way!" Justin exclaimed.

Elli, refusing to move, replied, "He's not going to hurt us. He saved Branda and me from the dean."

"He what?" Justin asked incredulously.

"You're not the only bloody hero around, Spaller," Derek replied, pinning Justin with a look.

Before Justin could reply with a scathing remark, Branda broke in. "It's true," she gasped, holding her side. "He stopped the dean from cutting my throat and from hurting Elli. He's on our side."

"And he's coming with us," Elli added, stepping slowly forward to face Justin.

"What are you talking about? He's the enemy, love! You can't just invite him to jump on board. Look at what he let happen to Branda."

The sight of her friend's torture-marked face made Elli pause. She knew how it looked, but she was not going to back down. "He saved our lives," she said with finality. "Branda's and mine. We're *not* leaving him here to die."

"Elli's right," Branda chimed in. "Derek saved us, and we owe him." Branda's raspy voice had struck a chord and Elli saw it on both Teddy and Justin's faces.

It was Teddy who let his power ebb away first. Stepping forward, he put a hand on Justin's shoulder, his Southern accent filled with reason as he spoke, "We don't have time for this. The dean could be headed this way now. We've got to leave."

"Fine. Let's get out of here, but this conversation is far from over," he said, his voice still gruff as his eyes returned to their normal gray color. An unreadable expression crossed Derek's face as Justin took Elli's hand.

Without another word, Teddy stepped forward and helped Derek with Branda. Together, the three of them began to move down the hall again with Justin and Elli behind. As they rushed once again down the hallway, Elli's thoughts seemed to move as quickly as her feet. Where was the dean? Why hadn't he come after them yet?

"Look, there's the double stairs," Teddy called back. "The door is at the bottom. We're almost out!"

"Fools! You can't get away from me. The girl is mine!" the dean's voice boomed from all around them, causing them to stumble. They barely kept their feet as a deafening rumble of power filled the hall and rushed past them down the stairs, dust flying in its wake. To their horror, as they stood on the landing between the two sets of stairs leading down, the slate-tiled floor at the bottom of the stairs began to lift. The sound of stone grinding on stone made chills run up and down Elli's spine. It was like a surreal nightmare as the black, gray, and brown streaked slate pieces cracked and began to connect to each other in mid-air, one piece overlapping with the next like some mad jigsaw puzzle. It took only a moment for it all to take shape before them.

"A dragon! Are you kidding me?" Branda shrieked as they all backed up slowly from the beast.

"And it's between us and the door," Derek shot back.

"Now what?" Elli asked in frustration as the dragon opened its jaws, revealing a hollowness behind sharp, stone teeth. She knew that in seconds the beast would reach for them. It would either swallow them whole or out-right impale them on its jagged teeth.

"There's nothing for it. Down the stairs!" Justin exclaimed.

"Did you happen to notice the eighteen-foot tall, rock dragon in front of us?" Derek yelled. His outburst seemed to break the delicate stalemate between them and the monster. In a flash, it lunged for them, its cavernous jaws open and it is black eyes piercing. They had seconds to react. The small distance they had put between themselves and it saved them as they were able to dart to the sides, Elli and Justin to the right, back towards the hallway opening, and the others to the left. Dust and small shards of broken slate rained down on them and the sounds of cracking wood from the railing and stairs filled their ears. Again and again it snapped its jaws at them.

Though there was no heat coming from it, Elli could almost feel its hot breath on her as she and Justin struggled to get away from the dragon's fangs; the beast seemed to only have eyes for them. The sound of snapping jaws was only overshadowed by the sound of the dragon's clawed feet and large, scaled belly breaking the right-side staircase as it stepped on them. Through the dust, she could see Teddy, Branda, and Derek. They were near the second set of stairs on the opposite wall, and she knew they had a chance of escape.

"Go!" Elli called to them.

"Not without you!" Teddy called back.

"We'll find another way out!" Justin yelled as he and Elli backed further into the hallway opening. Before anyone could react, the dragon's slate-tiled head reared back like a striking cobra and it lunged for them again. Instinct told them to dive forward out of the opening and back onto the landing, causing the dragon to knock its monstrous head into the roof of the hallway, cutting them off. Sharp slate pieces that made up the dragon's head broke off and rained down on them.

"Look!" Derek yelled, pointing as the neck of the dragon pulled back with a shake, revealing that parts of the face were missing, making the visage appear even more frightening due to its deformity. It seemed that, though the dean's magic could make the floor tile come to life, thankfully it could not change the brittleness of slate.

"Stop taking in the scenery and get out of here!" Justin yelled, pulling Elli to her feet while the dragon was momentarily dazed.

"Your concern is touching, Spaller, but I've got an idea," Derek retorted.

"So, you're gonna play the hero, huh. That's a change."

"Someone has to," Derek rebuffed and then pointed up, through the dust and chaos of the dragon, at the exposed beams overhead. "Those beams have to weigh a ton. We can crush this thing if we can loosen one of them." In a fluid motion he reached into his back pocket, pulled out a lighter, and ran it down the side of his jeans, igniting it. Pinning Justin with a look, his eyes turning a deep, burning red he added, "If you've got the nerve to fight back, that is."

With a flick of his wrist, Derek pulled the fire from the lighter and spreading his fingers wide, aimed it at the beam above the dragon's head. The fire struck home, igniting the

beam in a burst of flames. The monster, having no fear of the
fire overhead, lunged toward them again. They barely moved
out of the way in time.

"We've got to hold it in place, or this will never work!"
Branda exclaimed.

Looking around frantically, Elli saw the tipped over
devil's ivy plants on the main floor she'd noticed her first day
at Clandestine University, their pots shattered and the trellises
smashed to pieces. "Teddy! The plants! Help me!" she
screamed as she reached in her mind for her green magic.
Calling to the vines, she fed them her powers until, with years
of growth smashed into seconds, they were long and winding.
Her magic gave them strength far beyond their normal limits.
With Teddy's help and power feeding the plants too, she
wound the vines around the dragon until it began to lash back
and forth. Every time the razor-sharp slate sliced into a vine,
Elli and Teddy forced another to take its fallen brother's
place.

"That's it! Hold it tightly, love, and I'll help Blackwell
burn the beam quicker." Justin drew a fireball from his own
lighter and aimed his powers at the already burning beam at the
same time Derek threw another orb of flame at it. With the
combined force, the fire ate away at the two ends of the beam
with voracity. It took only seconds for the flames to weaken
the beams hold on the rafters. With a loud snap and groan, it
let loose.

The last thing Elli saw before Justin shoved her against
the wall and shielded her with his own body was the beam
hanging in mid-air for less than a heartbeat and then it was
falling. The dragon, still held by the vines, made one more
attempt to grab them before the beam landed. The sound of
slate tile cracking and the timber toppling down from above
was deafening. Dust, ash, and stone chips pelted Elli and the
others despite their best attempts to cover their bodies.

Once the sounds had dissipated, coughing from the dust,
Elli opened her eyes to find that the stairwell, landing, and
room below lay in shambles. The stained-glass window over

the door was gone and brightly colored glass twinkled in the rubble. Broken slate tiles lay in misshapen piles, punctuated by the occasional green leaf, and a fine covering of dust and stone pieces covered the splintered remains of the stairs. Small fires from the beam were burning in several corners of the once pristine, all-be-it gloomy, entrance way to Clandestine University.

With hesitation, Justin pulled away from her. Running his eyes over her to see if she was seriously hurt, he asked, "Are you alright?"

"Just a few cuts and bruises," she replied.

"And I'm okay, too, in case you were wondering," Derek replied, stepping through the cloud of dust toward them, Teddy and Branda behind him. All three looked as bedraggled as Elli and Justin, with small welts from flying debris marking their skin. Teddy's right eye looked swollen.

"You're alright?" Elli asked them.

"Never better," Branda said, cracking a smile. It would have been more convincing if she hadn't winced afterward. "You?"

"I'll live," Elli replied with her own grin.

Looking at her intently to see if she really was alright, Derek replied, "We need to get moving. They threw a lot of power into that dragon, but it will only take the Acolytes a few minutes to recover and if you think tile lizards are all they can summon, you're dead wrong. They can do things you've never dreamed of. I've seen it."

"And helped them along." Justin wrapped a protective arm around Elli's shoulders, pulling her closer to him. It was obvious that Derek had heard him but had decided to ignore the comment.

"Let's get out of here," Teddy said.

Carefully, using what was left of the stairs, railings, and banisters as foot and hand-holds in a ladder, they made their way to the door. It didn't take much strength to push it open as a large stone had struck it square in the center, bending the wrought-iron bands like putty and popping the rivets from the old oak. Once outside, Elli breathed a sigh of relief to see Cyn Dal and Page waiting for them. The sound of the running engine was music to her ears and the cool night air felt wonderful on her flushed skin.

The gravel crunched under their feet as they quickly made their way to the van.

"Branda!" Cyn Dal called, jumping out and hugging the tattooed girl who winced, but hugged back. "You're all right!"

"Takes more than that to keep me down," she replied, giving Cyn Dal a huge grin before Teddy helped her into the van's middle seat before climbing in, himself. Elli watched as Cyn Dal and Page's eyes grew large when they saw Derek walking up.

"What's he doing here?" Page asked, her voice weak but hostile even from where she sat in the back seat.

"Turning over a new leaf, apparently," Justin replied sarcastically, opening the driver's side door.

As Elli waited for Cyn Dal to climb into the back seat before following, she suddenly felt as if the air around her was thickening. Her vision began to grow hazy and tingles were spreading through her body. Her mind began to fill with images, and a strange feeling of being half-in and half-out of a premonition crept over her. She saw a stone basin divided into four parts; one part held water, another soil, a third fire, and the fourth smoke. Just outside the light created by the basin, she saw a group of figures encircling it. From the shapes of their shadows, Elli recognized the Acolytes even in the gloom, and she could feel a kind of wicked determination surrounding them. There was a flickering of power and a smell of wet ash as they began to mold their last effort at capturing Elli and her friends before they could get beyond the physical range of their power.

"Guys," Elli began, coming out of her trance to find that her senses weren't nearly as painful as they were when she was coming out of a full premonition, "I think they're sending something else our way. We'd better leave now!"

"I've got news for you," Derek replied as he looked over

his shoulder. Following his gaze, her heart skipped a beat. "It's already here." A swirling cloud began to form over the school, gaining speed as it spun.

"Get in!" Justin yelled, climbing behind the wheel and slamming the door. Elli quickly slid into the backseat while Derrick slammed the side door closed. The tires squealed and they sped off just as Derek closed the passenger door he'd just climbed through. Turning in her seat, Elli watched the cloud grow until it blocked the stars over the university roof. It seemed to be reaching out toward them with cruel, dagger-like fingers. In shock, Elli watched as the cloud began to chase them, breaking up into small, shiny pieces that caught what little light the moon gave off. It wasn't until one of the shiny pieces slammed into the back window, piercing it, that Elli realized what was chasing them.

"Leaves!" she breathed, watching as they rained down on them, their multi-colored bodies looking almost iridescent in the soft light of night.

"What?" Page asked, her eyes wide with terror.

"Razor sharp leaves! They'll cut us to pieces! Faster!" Elli exclaimed as the engine screamed. She bounced hard against Cyn Dal, who was being thrown against Page who sat on her opposite side, as Justin took a sharp curve. The adrenaline in her veins was singing as the horror chased them. To her terror, she realized that it wasn't just a forest of leaves, but the shapes were made of each element. Bright reddish-orange leaves left a trail of smoke as they pummeled the vehicle, burning the paint as they tried to pierce the fender wells and puncture the tires. Blue leaves turned into hail stones that shot at the windows, trying to smash their way in. Razor sharp yellow and green ones began to pummel the van's rear doors, lashing and ripping the metal.

"We can't outrun them!" Page cried, looking out the back window. "They're being uplifted by an air elemental!"

"Not just air," Elli said, pointing. "See the colors. They are made of other elements as well!"

"That explains why they can't get ahead of us and cut the

front tires. The other elements are heavy to carry. The leaves are waiting for us to make a mistake!" Cyn Dal's normally calm voice was high pitched with fear.

"Then we'll just have to outsmart them!" Teddy said, gripping the ceiling handle and front seat at the same time to keep from knocking into Branda.

"They're leaves! How do you expect us to outsmart them?" Derek asked, sarcastically.

"Hold on!" Justin yelled as hail and heavy leaf-shaped rain thumped on the roof and made seeing nearly impossible. The windshield wipers were madly whipping across the glass but only giving him a split second to see where he was going. Elli's heartbeats were keeping time with the speed of the wipers as she looked back again. The cloud of foliage was nearly on them. She could feel the back of the van lifting up and then setting down again as Justin gained another inch. Another leaf spider-webbed the glass of the back window. Elli could smell the acrid scent of acid and death.

"Elli, do something before we all die!" Derek yelled through gritted teeth.

"Like what?" she cried back as she slammed into the side of the van. "I'm up for any ideas!"

"You've got the power. Use it!"

"Leave her alone, Blackwell!" Justin hollered angrily as he jerked the wheel.

"Like hell! I don't want to die in this rust bucket being chased down like a rabbit. She's got all this power. It's time she used it. Come on, Elli!"

"I don't know what to do!" she yelled back, clenching her fists with anger and helplessness.

Derek whipped around in his seat to stare at her, his face hard. "Bull! Think!"

"I said leave her alone!" Justin shouted, his jaw so tight Elli thought it would snap in two.

"Justin, watch out!" Teddy yelled.

Chapter 6

Everything following Teddy's horrified exclamation was a blur to Elli later. She saw the ravine and heard Justin frantically pushing the brake pedal, but the van was speeding on so fast and the ground was so slick that there was no time to stop. She felt herself go over the edge and heard Page scream. There was a sick moment of emptiness under her as Elli sensed the depth of the ravine and the pungent smell of fear around her.

Out of instinct, she reached in her mind for something. Anything. She knew the leaves were right behind them. She had the mingled sensations of being propelled forward through the air and the fear of crashing into the opposite side wall of the narrow ravine. *Funny*, she thought in a moment of insane calm, *the ravine kind of looks like a knife cut.* Before her eyes, she watched as the cliff face opened up to reveal a kind of tunnel. She felt the jarring connection as the rubber wheels made contact with the rock and the sudden squealing of brakes as Justin brought the van to a stop just inside. Elli barely had time to register that she was in a small, bubble-like cave as a blast of wind rocked the vehicle. Dust and debris flew past them and slammed against the concave walls as they heard a sound like a train behind them, followed by a loud crash that echoed through the small area, making their ears hurt. As quickly as it had come, the noise stopped, leaving silence behind.

"What just happened?" Page asked, her eyes wide with shock and her body locked with some kind of paralysis.

Elli realized that she didn't feel much better. Her mind was spinning, and she felt light headed. The old leather seat cushions seemed rough on her palms, and the light that glared back at her from the reflection of the headlights on the light-colored rock of the cave made her eyes hurt.

"Is everyone okay?" Justin asked, swiveling around in his seat and looking at them.

"Bloody brilliant!" Branda said, grinning barbarically. "Can we do it again?" Her dangerous sense of humor was enough to break the stillness as everyone laughed, thankful to be alive.

The hinges of the driver and passenger side doors squeaked as Justin and Derek climbed out. Piling out of the van, Elli realized that despite the euphoria of being alive, her legs were shaky, almost wobbly. When she stood, her eyes met Derek's for a moment. They were a mixture of amazement and cool conceit. Suddenly angry at him and his easy arrogance that he put on like a coat whenever he wanted, Elli walked around the van, determined not to show him her weakness.

"Are you really okay?" Justin asked, as he followed her.

"Yeah. Fine," she replied, giving him a watery smile and then turning to look out the cave mouth to avoid his gaze. The cave, itself, wasn't as perfectly round as she had thought at first. The floor was level, like someone had taken a large ice cream scoop out of the cliff face and then smoothed the hole left behind. Outside the opening, Elli could see the opposite wall of the ravine.

"Wow!" Cyn Dal said, coming up to stand next to them. "Were we lucky that this cave was here or what?"

"Yeah, lucky. Now, how do we get out of here?" Derek questioned from his position next to the van.

"Always the ray of sunshine, aren't you?" Page asked.

"Can't you be a little happy that we're still alive after that? I mean come on. Take a moment and smell the roses!"

"Hey, I'll smell the roses when we've got about two hundred miles between us and Clandestine. Besides, they may have run out of steam for the moment, but you can be damn sure they're already recharging," he retorted, ignoring Page's eye roll. "So, I repeat, how do we get out of here?"

"Getting out isn't our only problem," Teddy added.

"He's right. We have to decide what to do once we're out. We need some kind of direction," Cyn Dal reasoned.

"And we have to think of some kind of transportation since the van has had it," Justin stated, gesturing toward it. Turning to examine the vehicle, Elli noticed for the first time how scratched and dented it really was. The back window was busted out and several long, nasty gouges ran along the roof, surprising her that the leaves hadn't broken through in the end.

"It *is* a little conspicuous," Branda added as she leaned against the hood of the van.

"Anyone have any ideas?" Derek asked, his arms crossed.

"We could try opening the box Elli had a premonition about," Page offered, pulling her pack from the floor of the back seat. She walked to the front of the van where the headlights still shinned and took the small, black box from the bag. Chills swept up and down Elli's arms, causing goose bumps to rise, as she saw for the first time the box that had haunted her underwater premonition. She felt compelled as she walked toward Page to take the box, but as her hand reached out for it, she had an equal feeling of fear and anxiety about touching the black wood and pulled her hand back.

"Oh, that stupid thing," Derek stated sarcastically, his face all plains and shadows in the dim light. "Clandestine's had it ever since I've known him, but he's never been able to figure out how to open it. He's tried everything from 'abracadabra' to a crowbar, but nothing works. You'll never be able to open it, Pandora."

With Derek's cynicism compelling her to prove him

wrong, the box still in Page's hands, Elli placed her thumbs under the lid and pushed, expecting to meet resistance but finding none. It popped open easily to Derek's surprise. Letting it fall open all the way, Elli peered inside, her heart beating wildly, only to find it empty.

"There's nothing in it!" Page exclaimed.

"Impossible," Justin said in disbelief, standing behind Elli to look for himself.

As all six of her friends crowded around her to see what was inside the box, Elli had a strange sense that something was about to happen. Her fingers began to tingle, and she felt a rush of wind whip around her legs. The headlights began to flicker wildly. There was a smell of burning beech wood and wet earth in the air.

"Oh, God! The Acolytes are going for round three!" Branda yelled over the wind.

"No! It's coming from the box!" Page hollered back, dropping it to the floor as they all backed away. As soon as the box hit the stone floor, a burst of light flew from it, hitting the ceiling and then raining down on them. Before she could react, Justin pressed his body against hers to shield her from it, turning his back to the brightness. After a moment, the wind dropped away, leaving them momentarily stunned. In the silence, Elli looked up into Justin's gray eyes and nodded that it was okay to let her go. As he did so, she noticed that her friends were also beginning to look around. Teddy, who had moved closer to Cyn Dal to protect her from the wind, was taking her small hand in his large, mahogany brown one. Page was shaking dust from her red curls while Branda was emerging from the van. Derek, who had moved much closer during the blast, was straightening himself as well. Elli had the odd sensation that he may have been reaching for her but stopped.

It was then that she looked at the box. A thin ray of light was shooting from it, hitting the ceiling and then raining back down like a fountain. As her gaze was drawn to it, Elli felt in her heart that everything was going to be okay now. Her apprehensions and fears were gone, washed away in the blue-white brilliance that now shown from the open box on the floor. She felt the need to step forward just as her friends must have. They formed a circle around the glow, standing almost shoulder to shoulder.

After only a second or two, the light began to pulse like a heartbeat and in the center, something began to take shape, twisting the light until a disembodied head floated in the stream. The face was kind, almost young despite the short, white beard that flowed from its chin. Elli felt a shock when she realized that she was looking into eyes very much like her own vivid green ones. A smile flickered over the face, almost in response to her realization.

"I am prowde of thou, chyldryn. Thou haue don wel," the head said. The language sounded almost familiar to the group, but not so much that they could understand it. The telepathic web buzzed with confusion, except for one person.

"It's Old English," Cyn Dal explained, quietly. It was spoken around Merlin's time, and it only makes sense that if this is Merlin's image, it would use his language.

"Can you understand it?" Justin asked.

"I think so. English hasn't been spoken like this in a few thousand years. I think he said, 'I am proud of you, my children. You have done well.'" As Merlin continued on, Cyn Dal's voice seemed to fade away until it was almost as if Merlin was speaking directly to them.

"You've found the box that contains my last wishes, but more importantly, you've found each other. You are the key to saving this world from annihilation by dark forces that were alive even in my time. Evil sleeps but does not die. I am sorry that this task has come to you who are still so young, but I learned long ago to not question the choices fate makes. I have done all that I can by splitting my power amongst a few in hopes that enough will be there for you to use in this fight. The book that was laid to rest with this box, the second of my histories, should give you aid as I have written down what prophecies have come to me concerning your destiny. I have encoded them for protection, but brilliance and selflessness will light the way. I have left only one other talisman for this battle. You must find the crystal, my children. I have hidden it well, but you are of my blood and power. The crystal will call to you, and you must follow wherever it may lead."

Merlin paused for a moment, seeming to collect his thoughts before looking full force on Elli. "My daughter," he began, his voice troubled, "I know you are here as you are the only person who could have opened this box. It is to you that I bequeath my remaining power, including the skill of divination. I wish with all my heart that I could spare you the road you must now take with your new-found family. Alas, you are truly my last hope. In the end, after the fight has ensued, it will be your choice that decides the final outcome of this battle. I have only one piece of advice. Trust your heart and listen to the words another will write one day, far from now, in a time of strange costumes. I am sorry that I cannot be there, my daughter, to help you further. Time is our enemy in all things, and mine has nearly run out. You must find my crystal, the one you have dreamed of, but beware who places it upon your brow at the appointed hour for his will be the side your power will be meant for. One hand kind, one grasping, daughter. Remember that and trust your heart, child. Good luck, my children, and farewell."

As Merlin finished speaking, the blue light began to pulse with energy and then flared out, striking each of them like a sonic wave from an explosion. The feeling of energy bubbled in her veins, making Elli feel wonderfully carefree. Just as quickly as it had come, the flare flickered and faded, leaving her and her friends standing once again in the glow from the van's headlights.

Taking in her surroundings, Elli realized that her friends looked different. Justin was quiet but determined, his gray eyes flashing. Page seemed to stand a little taller. Teddy had an air of strength and confidence while Cyn Dal's serenity wafted around her like an aura. Derek, standing a little outside the circle, was as still as if he'd been turned to stone, his eyes dark but lost in thought. Perhaps the most amazing transformation was found in Branda. She stood on her own two legs, her head tall and proud. Her skin was clear of all bruises and abrasions; only her ragged clothing was left to tell the tale of her torture at the hands of the Acolytes.

It was then that Elli realized her own wounds no longer stung; glancing down at her arms which had been cut and bloodied by flying debris, she realized that they were healed, not even a scar remaining. It was true of the others as well; even Teddy's swollen eye was mended. Bending down, she picked up the box only to find that it fell to pieces in her hands.

"It's wasting away now that the power in it is gone," Justin said, wrapping his arm around her waist. Smiling a bittersweet smile, Elli let all that was left of the box fall to the floor where it was blown away by some unfelt wind.

"Now what?" Teddy asked.

"Well, Merlin said that the crystal would call to us, but I don't hear anything," Page said, shrugging her shoulders.

"I don't think he meant it like that," Branda replied. "I think it is more like we'd feel the direction to take."

"Okay. So, does anyone 'feel' which way we should go?" Page asked.

"Elli does," Derek said, the sureness of his voice making them all turn to stare at him.

"What do you mean?" Cyn Dal asked.

Derek leaned against the car, crossing his arms in one easy motion, his head cocked to one side. He paused as if he were about to say something, but changed his mind and said, "I only mean that she's Merlin's descendant. If anyone would know, she would."

"He's right," Teddy said. "What do you think, Elli?"

"I think we don't have much choice."

"Wait a minute," Cyn Dal said as she crawled through the open driver's side door. After the momentary sound of rustling papers and the slamming of the glove compartment, she reemerged holding a map. "Use this. It might help like the blue prints did for finding Branda." Taking the map from the girl's outstretched hand with a small smile of thanks, Elli spread it out over the heavily scratched hood of the van, suppressing a shudder at the all-too-recent memory of the Acolyte attack. Feeling a warm hand on her shoulder, she turned, meeting a pair of gray eyes that told her without words to be careful.

Winking at him with a confidence she didn't really feel, she pulled away from his embrace to once again stare at the map. Closing her eyes, she sought for the cluster of jewels in her mind as she rhythmically breathed in and out, concentrating on the crystal she'd seen in her visions, Merlin's crystal. Once she had the image in her mind, she lifted her hands and began to let them slowly hover over the map, moving from grid to grid, repeating the question, "*Where are you?*" After several passes with no luck, Elli opened her eyes. Confused, she gritted her teeth and tried again, repeating the steps she used to find Branda. When a premonition still refused to surface, she let her hands drop to her sides with frustration, an irritated sigh escaping her lips.

"What's wrong?" Justin asked.

"I don't know. I can't seem to find it. It's like I feel this tickle in my brain, and I know that the knowledge is there, but it's just out of reach. I don't understand," she said, annoyed at her own inability.

"Well, Merlin did say that the stone was protected," Page said, placing her elbows on the hood to get a better look at the map. "Maybe he made it so it couldn't be scried."

"Yeah, but he also said that anyone of his blood and power could find it. No one is more that than Elli," Teddy added.

"But if he put strong wards on it so no one person could find it, it would be like the same thing," Branda added, running a hand through her red-tipped, spiked hair as she thought.

"What about the book?" Cyn Dal asked. "Maybe he left a treasure map or something inside?"

"Not hardly. The Acolytes would have discovered it a

long time ago," Justin began. "Besides, Merlin said that the book only contained prophecies. He didn't mention anything about a map."

The sound of laughter made them all turn once again to Derek who had not moved from his careless position.

"What's so funny?" Branda asked, glaring.

"You! You're all acting like this is some stupid brain teaser when the answer is so disgustingly simple."

"Okay, out with it. What are we missing?" Page questioned, crossing her arms in defiance.

"Elli's just tired. She isn't a bloody crystal ball. After everything that's happened tonight," Derek began to tick the items off on his fingers, the movement exaggerated and sarcastic, "the premonitions, fighting off the dean, binding the dragon, the cave –"

"The cave?" Page stated, interrupting him. "What do you mean the cave?"

"She created it, of course. Are you really that stupid?"

"What!" Elli exclaimed, unable to control herself. "I didn't do this. That's impossible!" She could feel her stomach clench and her hands begin to shake.

"Why?" he asked.

"Because, because... it just is! How could I have done something like this? It's just too big!"

"Have you forgotten who you are, Lady Allison? You're Merlin's successor. You've got the power to move the planets if you chose to do so. Do you think that digging a little hole in the ground is anything for you? Besides, what do you think the odds are of us landing in such a perfectly hollowed-out cave at the exact level with where we should have crashed? A million to one? A billion?"

"Leave her alone, Blackwell," Justin grumbled, stepping toward Derek, his eyes snapping with an inner flame. Justin may as well have been a part of the scenery for all the attention Derek gave him.

"Finding a little crystal should be an easy task for you."

"I said leave her alone!" Elli watched as Justin's hands

connected with Derek's shoulders in a violent shove. In one fluid motion, Derek was face to face with Justin, his lean body emanating danger like a downed power-line.

"Yeah, Derek. You'd better bloody well leave her alone," Branda added, coming to stand just behind Justin. Though she wasn't looking at them, Elli felt Cyn Dal, Teddy and Page tense, ready for anything. The distrust and anxiety were so strong that Elli almost felt like she was suffocating.

"Do you think the Acolytes are going to leave her alone? They'll kill her if they get the chance just so no one else can have her," Derek snapped. His dark eyes began to pulse with anger and his fists were clenched so hard Elli was sure the bones would break through the skin. The whole scene reminded her of scorpions poised to fight, their stingers deadly sharp.

"I won't let that happen! No one is going to touch her as long as I have a breath of life in me," Justin snarled.

"And that goes for the rest of us, too," Teddy added, his voice determined.

"You idiots think I'm the enemy. Well, fine! I'm the bloody enemy. I didn't join up with you for my health. I came for Elli and I'll do anything –"

The dull thudding of bone on soft flesh resounded in the cave as Justin's fist connected with Derek's mouth.

"Stop it!" Elli exclaimed, slamming her fists down on the hood of the car as she yelled. She felt the reverberation go up her arm and then a sudden release as a premonition flooded her mind. Sun set. A fence of steel and wood. Water and gulls. Clocks ticking. Sun set. One person, two faces. Blank. Nothing behind the eyes. Sun set. A barking dog with dark brown ears. An hour glass....

Elli gasped as she fell back into herself. She could feel her whole body shaking as she opened her eyes to see the too-brightly colored map before her. Her hands were still balled up into fists, but only the left hand lay on the map itself.

"On the west side. The direction of the setting sun. We have to make it to the ocean," she whispered, her voice raspy.

"Elli? Are you okay?" Page asked, laying a cool hand on her arm.

"I'm fine. Just a little dizzy. Maybe Derek's right. Too much in one night," she said, giving her friend a reassuring smile. Looking up, she found Derek and Justin staring at her intently, waiting. "I know which way to go. It's time to leave."

Chapter 7

The pack felt heavy on her back, but it was a comforting weight as she followed the others across the moor, the sweet smell of heather drifting up from under their feet. It had been no easy task getting all seven of them down from the cave. Even though Justin had packed a rope in the trunk along with all their other belongings, in their tired condition it was quite a task to lower all their backpacks and then themselves down the cliff face. But perhaps the most difficult part had been convincing Justin to let Derek come along. Elli had reasoned that if they left him there, he would die. He had nowhere to go since the dean would surely kill Derek if he found him. It took some persuasion, but she finally convinced him that Derek could be useful. Besides, he'd saved her life. Justin hadn't been happy with her which is why he chose to keep his distance, walking at the head of the group, his back tense and angry as he ignored her. *Fine,* she thought as she side-stepped a rock in her path, *I can ignore him, too.*

Elli knew they were all exhausted, but she also knew that they couldn't stop to rest yet. She felt something driving them along. Though she wasn't sure what they were rushing towards, it was something important.

"I was wondering," Branda began, falling back to talk to her in private, "what are you up to?"

"What do you mean?" she asked, peering into the girl's sky-blue eyes. In her new, clean clothing, Branda's torture at the hands of the Acolytes seemed just been a bad dream.

"You know exactly what I bloody well mean," she said, nodding her head toward Derek who walked not exactly beside Justin, but close enough so they could keep an eye on each other. "Why did you let Derek come along?"

"You were there. You saw him save our lives. I'm just returning the favor," she replied, keeping her voice low.

"Yeah, I did, but when I stood up for him at Clandestine, I didn't think you were going to invite him to help us find Merlin's crystal. He still can't be trusted. It would have been better to let him fend for himself after we escaped."

"And then we'd be no better than the Acolytes," she rationalized, trying to make Branda understand.

"Maybe," she said, pausing for a moment. "But I just don't trust him. Promise me that once we find a safe place, we leave him behind. I don't think it's a good idea for him to go with us all the way."

"If we find a safe place for him," she replied, and they walked along in silence, each lost in thought. It would have been difficult for her to explain to Branda exactly why she felt Derek had to go with them. Though she had her own doubts, there could be no question about how many times he'd saved her life. What if Derek was trying to redeem himself? It wasn't right to deny him the chance.

"Look!" Cyn Dal called, pointing excitedly, her voice bringing Elli out of her reverie. Just at the base of the hill, Elli saw a small railway station and a maze of tracks. What drew her eye, however, were not the piles of rock and other goods waiting to be shipped, but a loaded cargo train on tracks leading west. It looked as though the train was preparing to disembark.

"That's it!" she cried. "The fence made of steel and wood. It's a railroad track! We have to get on that train."

"Wait a minute. Doesn't anyone find it a little coincidental that we found exactly what we need to continue on?" Branda asked.

"I don't care as long as we don't have to walk to the shore. It's over a hundred miles away, and I'm exhausted," Page said, repositioning her backpack.

"I say we try it," Teddy said.

"And what does our fearless leader think?" Derek asked, his dark eyes skeptical.

Ignoring the condescension in Derek's voice, Justin pinned Elli with a look, the first he'd given her since their descent down the cliff. He was silent for a moment as he stared at her, his face still showing a slight trace of anger, but the set of his mouth betraying the decision he was about to make. "If Elli saw the train in her vision, I say we trust it. If we're wrong, we'll have lost nothing but time."

In silent agreement, they descended the hill, making their way to the station. It was slow going as they tried not to attract the attention of any of the railway workers, ducking behind piles of stone and stacks of pallets, trying not to trip over the maze of steel tracks that littered the ground.

"Wait!" Justin whispered as they ducked between two rows of rusty cargo boxes. Peering over his shoulder, Elli could see that the train was less than ten yards away, but it was going to be tricky to get to it. There was nothing to hide behind and way too many workers around.

"Look," Teddy said softly, pointing toward the tail end of the train. "It looks like the fifth box from the end is just carrying crates of food. There should be enough room for all of us in there."

"Yeah, but how do we get there?" Elli asked, chewing her lip with anxiety.

"Page? Do you think you could whip us up some fog?" Cyn Dal asked, her brown eyes intently watching the workers walking back and forth across the yard.

"No problem," the pixie-like girl replied, closing her eyes as she began to breathe deeply. Elli felt a kind of shimmer in the air as Page reopened her eyes, revealing the gold-ish color they had become. Looking past the train, she saw a thick cloud bank begin to roll toward them, flowing across the hillside like a wave of grayness to lay heavily over the station, blinding everyone, especially the grumbling workmen.

"Brilliant," Justin began, peering through the gloom, "let's go. One at a time. More than that will attract attention no matter how thick the fog is. I'll go first." Reaching over, he lightly touched her face, his annoyance forgotten for the moment. *"Be safe, love,"* he said, a silent message meant for only her.

"You, too," Elli replied, smiling her best fearless smile despite the butterflies in her stomach. With that, Justin disappeared in a swirl of smoke. She strained her eyes to see into the cloud but to no avail. Page's fog was just too dense. Even though they'd had no sign that he was in trouble, Elli felt like her heart was in her throat. "This is taking way too long," she whispered to Cyn Dal who knelt beside her.

"Give him a chance. He's only been gone for a minute or two." The reassurance in her voice was like a balm to Elli's frayed nerves. Mentally telling herself to calm down, she tried to take a few deep breaths.

"Okay, I'm in. Come on," Justin called, telepathically.

"Page, you next," Elli said, determined to make sure all of her friends were safely on the train before following. About to disagree, Page saw the look on her face and decided not to argue. Re-adjusting her backpack, she walked into the wall of cloud in search of the train followed shortly by Cyn Dal, Teddy, and Branda until only Elli and Derek remained.

"It's your turn," Elli whispered, peering once again into the fog.

"I don't think so," he replied, catching her eye. "I want to be last in case you need a diversion to make it the rest of the way. Besides, I'm not leaving you here alone. What if our hiding place is discovered?"

"Exactly. That's why you're going. We may be running out of time already," she reasoned, crossing her arms.

"And how much time are you wasting by arguing with me when you know I'm going to win? I can be just as stubborn as you. And you'd better take that backpack off and carry it. You don't want it snagging on anything as you go." The set of his jaw and the glint in his eyes told her that he was being candid. Sighing heavily, she closed her eyes, took the canvas bag in her hands, whispered a prayer and set off. The fog swallowed her the moment she stepped out from between the stacked cars, the moisture of it coating her skin in a clammy dew. Keeping her breathing slow and easy, she tried to remember the exact direction that the boxcar was in.

Straight out and to the left, she told herself as she stepped over railroad ties.

"Hey, Angus!" a voice called beside her, too close for comfort. Freezing, Elli felt her throat tighten.

"I'm over here. Bloody fog! Can't see a thing!" a man hollered off to her right, in the exact opposite direction of the original yell. The sound of crunching gravel made Elli's skin crawl when she realized that the footsteps were coming toward her. Steeling herself, she thought frantically – *The stacked cars are closer. If I just turn around slowly, I should be able to make it back there.* Elli turned quietly on her heel and began to make her way back as quickly as she could, her heart pounding loudly in her ears, the fog blinding her, her arms gripping her pack to her chest like a shield. Everything looked the same as she hurried along, afraid to make any noise. After a few more steps, Elli had the sickening feeling that she should have already come upon the rows of stacked railway cars.

Perfect, I'm lost, she thought to herself, her mind rushing with images of what would happen to her if she were caught trespassing. Biting her lip, she tried to make out images in the fog, but it was useless. The heaviness settled around her, opaque as a lead plate. Deciding that the only sensible thing to do was to keep going, she took a few more steps, trying to find something she recognized from her earlier look around the yard to help guide her in the right direction. Balling her hands into fists around her pack's material, she stepped further into the unknown.

"Well, well, look what I found!" a voice called from beside her, stopping Elli in mid-stride, her heart skipping a beat as she saw a disembodied hand reach toward her through the mist and grab her arm while a second one smothered her scream. "Gotcha!"

Chapter 8

"Stop it, Elli! It's me!" Derek hissed, cutting through the panic that had clouded her mind as she tried to pummel him with her backpack. She stopped struggling as he pulled her toward a stack of pallets piled in a kind of 'U' shape. Only when he was sure that she wouldn't scream did he feel safe removing his hand from her mouth. Turning her around, Elli saw that his dark eyes were framed with worry lines. "I'm glad I found you before someone else did."

"Me, too. I thought for sure that man was going to see me. I nearly had a heart attack." Pausing, Elli let her backpack fall to the ground as she tried to ignore the heat from his hands seeping through the arms of her shirt. "How did you find me?"

Smiling, he gently squeezed her arm. "I'm part blood hound." The sensation sent surprising tingles across her skin. His eyes were so dark, like two pin-points of night sky, and a lock of unruly hair fell across his forehead, softening his handsome features. Elli fought the need to touch his lips with her fingers, a need that confused yet compelled her.

"*Elli! Where are you? The train is about to leave!*" Justin yelled, his telepathic voice ringing in her mind, making her back away from Derek as if he were on fire, the strange connection she'd felt gone.

"What happened?" Derek asked, taking her hand in his in an attempt to draw her back to him.

"The train is leaving. We've got to hurry!"

"Let's go," he said, hefting her bag with his free hand. Following him through the gloom, Elli felt herself beginning to worry that they wouldn't make it in time.

"Hurry, Derek!" she whispered, feeling her heart race. The sight of the open boxcar door and Justin reaching for her was a sudden relief. Out of the corner of her eye, she saw Teddy haul Derek up just as the wheels began to spin, trying to find grip on the steel spur. Once inside, Elli's legs gave out, and she thankfully collapsed on a pile of flour sacks as Justin slammed the door shut.

"What took you so long? We were scared to death that you'd been caught!" Page said, taking a seat on a crate marked 'mushrooms.'

"Elli decided to go for a walk in the fog and meet some of the locals. She'd be their guest right now if I hadn't gone after her," Derek said, the sarcasm dripping from his lips as he tossed her bag down, the softness he'd shown a few minutes ago disappearing like smoke in the wind. Glaring at him, Elli decided that the next time he made her have even the slightest feeling toward him, she'd kick him in the leg.

"At least you're safe now," Justin said. "Thanks for getting her out of there, Blackwell." His voice was gruff but sincere.

"My pleasure," he replied, catching Elli's eye and winking, grinning at her anger.

Before she could snap at the two of them about being able to take care of herself, Branda broke in. "I don't know about you, but I'm exhausted."

"Yeah," Justin began, looking around and seeing the dark circles under everyone's eyes and their shaky appearance, little wonder after last night plus traipsing across the countryside, "I think we could all do with some sleep."

"And food," Page said, eyeing the crates and stacks around her.

"There are some apples in the corner," Teddy said, opening a bag and tossing one to each of them. "This should hold us over."

After eating a few apples and licking the sticky juice from their fingers, everyone settled down to sleep. Curling up next to Justin on their flour-sack bed, her head on his chest, Elli couldn't help but feel the rightness of being in his arms. The moment with Derek behind the fog-enshrouded pallets seemed like a dream; here was reality, with Justin.

Content and relaxed, she looked over her friends. Cyn Dal and Teddy had chosen a pile of empty sacks to sleep on, his arm slung protectively over her. Page was curled up on her own stack of flour, her backpack as a pillow. Branda was sprawled on some bags that appeared to contain sugar, appearing as comfortable as if she were in a feather bed. It was only Derek who had made his bed as far away from the group as he could, stretching out on the floor, his back against sacks of salt. Looking at his face, Elli realized that he was staring at her, his eyes flashing in the sunlight that peeped through the slits in the wooden door. His expression was unreadable, but she had the strange feeling that he was thinking about her, almost calling her with his eyes. Still angry with him for his earlier comments, she turned her mind from him and the strange connection that seemed to hover around them once again.

With Justin's strong arms as a protective blanket, she closed her eyes and breathed in his scent deeply as she sent a private message to him, "*I love you.*" She could feel Justin smile as he returned the message, stroking her hair, running it through his fingers until they both fell asleep listening to the hypnotic sounds of the train.

***

Bang... bang... bang... The loud noises woke Elli with a

start, her heart pounding, fear-sweat drenching her. Holding her breathe, she looked around only to find that everyone was still asleep. Justin lay silently beside her, his hair tousled, his chest rising and falling rhythmically. *Bang... bang... bang...*

Elli sat, listening to the repetitive sound, waiting for the others to wake. When no one stirred, she crawled from her flour-sack bed, careful not to disturb anyone, and stepped toward the boxcar door. All was darkness on the other side. *We must have slept the entire day away*, she thought, jumping when the loud banging sound repeated.

Looking down at her feet, she noticed for the first time that Derek wasn't where she'd last seen him, the indentations made by his shoulders in the salt sacks the only evidence of where he'd lain. It was then that Elli had a sinking feeling in her stomach.

Oh, my God! Derek must be outside! He can't get back in! Reaching for the handle, she slid the door open and screamed as the slate dragon's mouth opened towards her, the dean's eyes shining out from the once-empty sockets.

***

Sitting straight up, her heart in her throat, Elli saw the bright sunlight streaming in from the door that someone had been opened slightly to allow for more light. The monster was gone, leaving only a shivering sensation behind. Her friends were all up, busily working on different projects. Teddy and Branda were cutting apples up with a pocket knife. Justin was pouring over the map that they had taken from the car. Page was stirring something in a small camp pot over a steno burner, her bright red curls piled on top of her head with a rubber band. Derek had retreated to the door, starring outside as if he were searching the horizon. *Or just being anti-social*, she thought, crawling from her nest to sit next to Cyn Dal who was busily looking through the dean's notebook and the mysterious history that they had pilfered the night before.

"Why didn't you guys wake me?" Elli asked, pulling a

brush from her bag to try and untangle her long hair, wishing deeply that there was a bathtub handy.

"Justin said to let you sleep. After last night, he said you deserved it," she replied, her almond eyes smiling.

"Was I wrong?" Justin sat down on an adjoining crate, the map still clutched in his hands.

"No. I appreciate it, really," she said, leaning in to kiss him good morning.

"Hmmm. A satisfactory thank-you, if I do say so myself," Justin said as they pulled apart, wiggling his eyebrows lecherously. Giving him a playful push on the shoulder, Elli smiled, a slight blush making her cheeks rosy.

"So, have you figured out how to read that thing yet?" Derek interrupted as he gestured at the book, having left his secluded corner to hover over them.

"Not exactly. The book is written in Latin, but it's a strange form of Latin that I've never seen before. What I don't understand is why it would be written in Latin at all. Merlin would have used Old English."

"Well, the Romans did inhabit Britain for a long time, and it *is* possible that he picked up some Latin," Justin explained, leaning in to have a closer look at the book. "But I have no idea why it looks so strange."

"What does Clandestine say in his notes?" Derek asked, leaning against the wall with his hands stuffed in his pockets.

"Not much. It's just notes mostly on how to open the box that contained Merlin's message. It seems he tried for years to get it open and even resorted to some pretty desperate measures. Listen to this." Cyn Dal flipped through the pages of the leather-covered notebook until she found the one she wanted. "Here it is. '*March 14, 2008. I've tried every incantation I can think of to open the box that was discovered in the ruins but to no avail. It remains stubbornly shut to all my advances. I ordered B. to use acid on the seal. With luck, the chemical won't harm whatever is inside.*' She paused, turning the page before continuing. "'*March 15, 2008. The acid was useless! It may as well have been water! I am convinced that it contains some type of key for reading Merlin's history. If only I could find a way to break into it. If only the child would materialize for that matter.'"*

"Is there anything else?" Justin asked.

"There are a few more pages on how he tried different techniques on the seal. He even tried chiseling through the lid of the box to get a peek at what was inside, but something made the chisel shatter into a million pieces."

"Now *that's* desperation," Elli stated.

"Breakfast!" Page said, cheerily breaking in as she handed tin plates containing oatmeal and apples around.

While they all ate, sitting around the book, Elli let her mind drift, her thoughts wondering what the strange words that were Latin, but weren't Latin meant. An image of her mother popped into her thoughts. Elli smiled as she remembered how beautiful she had been. Long, flowing dark hair and sparkling green eyes, both of which she'd given to her daughter. Her face was always slightly tanned from the overhanging sun on dig sites, and she wore a vanilla scented perfume that would waft around her like a cloud whenever Elli would hug her. Whenever she wasn't digging in the dirt for bits of pottery, she was writing. She'd always wanted to publish, but never got the chance before she died. Her handwriting was lovely, scrolling, but illegible because she used her own personal short-hand –

"Wait! I've got it!" she exclaimed with excitement, dropping her spoon on her plate with a clang.

"What?" Branda asked, sitting yoga-style on a crate labeled 'canned asparagus,' her elbows on her knees, her empty plate beside her.

"It is Latin, but Merlin's own personal version of it. That's why we can't read it!"

"That's great, but how does that help us?" Teddy wondered, the apple slice he'd been about to eat forgotten.

"I'm not sure," Cyn Dal began. "If I had a point of reference... like a word or a phrase to go by, maybe I could translate the book."

"What was it that Merlin said before he went 'poof'?

Brilliance and something would light the way," Page said.

"Selflessness," Branda added. "He said that brilliance and selflessness would light the way."

"More riddles! This is a waste of time," Derek said, his tone steeped in annoyance, stealing some of Elli's delight at her discovery.

"Hey, no one begged you to come," Justin replied, standing, his old hatred toward Derek rekindled despite last night's show of good faith.

"Back off, Spaller. I'm in no mood." Derek kept his voice low, almost dangerous sounding, like a warning hiss from a snake.

"Why don't you just drop dead, you wanker!" Branda said, standing face to face with Derek, her blue eyes narrowed and her upper lip curled back. In slow motion, Elli watched as Justin shoved Branda out of the way, the tall girl barely catching herself as she stumbled over a crate. It seemed as if even the phoenix and dragon tattooed on her shoulder seethed in anger.

"No one asked you to butt in," Justin snarled, his fists clenched, spitting hatred at Branda.

"And no one asked you to act like our fearless leader!" Page added, her eyes snapping.

"Oh, shut up, you bloody little know-it-all!" Justin threw back.

"Screw you!" Branda hollered, her fist swinging through the air, connecting with Justin's jaw.

"Don't hit him!" Page screamed.

"I'll do what I bloody well want!" Branda replied, glaring at the fiery-topped Page.

"Why don't you just stay out of this, Page?" Derek said, his fists pulled up. "You won't catch me off guard this time, Spaller!"

"Why don't you all just sit down and shut up! You're acting like a bunch of idiots," Teddy said, his usually sweet face twisted in anger as he shoved Page down. A small scream of pain rang out as her leg was pinched between two crates.

Cyn Dal dropped the book on the floor, her cloud of serenity gone as she began berating Teddy and screaming at Justin whose eyes began to pulse red as he rubbed his sore chin.

"Knock it off, you guys!" Elli cried, standing as the scene grew more surreal by the moment. "What's wrong with you?"

"Oh, they can't hear you, my girl," a voice hissed behind her, a voice she recognized from the make-up room. The same voice that had stood outside her door on her first night at Clandestine University. *Snake.* "They're too busy wanting to kill each other to pay any attention to you. Or to me for that matter." Whipping around, Elli found only the slatted planks of the boxcar wall. "Looking for me?" Snake said, off to her right. But when she turned, she once again found only wall. "How about here?" Nothing.

Angry and frustrated, Elli shouted, "Show yourself or are you only good at hiding in shadows like a coward?"

"Now, now, it isn't polite to speak to your elders that way." A bright flash of light filled the car, causing Elli to throw her arm up to protect herself out of reflex. The strange smell of ozone and burnt sugar invaded her senses when she lowered her arm. As the spots in her vision cleared, Elli noticed that her friends were motionless, like living statues. Derek and Justin each held a ball of fire in their hands, ready to strike the other down. Branda, a savage snarl across her face, had Cyn Dal by the hair. Teddy and Page were glaring each other down, pure hatred glinting in their eyes. It was frightening how much loathing was still visible despite the lack of movement. But perhaps the strangest thing was the man walking among her friends like a visitor in an art museum, stopping here and there, smiling at the macabre exhibit.

"Dean Clandestine," she said, surprised at how steady her voice was despite the fear-adrenaline pumping through her veins. Perhaps she should have been astonished that he had been the snake-like voice that had plagued her days at Clandestine University, but Elli was way beyond shock after her previous night's experiences.

"We meet again, Miss Wafe." The dean bowed

mockingly, his form clad in a black robe with a red cord hanging from the waist, his salt-and-peppered hair uncovered. "It is always a pleasure to –" The dean paused, his brown eyes amused as he watched Elli gather power around herself to strike. "I wouldn't do that my dear. You might harm your bickering friends." Like a hologram in a sci-fi film, the dean stepped through the piles of food stuff as if they weren't there. "Besides, as you can see for yourself, I'm not exactly in the flesh."

Releasing the power she had been gathering, Elli glared at the dean. "This is your fault, isn't it?"

"Guilty. It is amazing what you can accomplish by playing on a person's emotions. And the freezing part? It adds a special touch; don't you think? It took my colleague over a year to perfect the art of using air in such a way, to bind the body, to astral project..." He paused long enough to nonchalantly gesture at himself, before continuing, "and to influence emotion." The pride in his voice made Elli's stomach turn, as did his sudden frown. "Sadly though, it doesn't seem to work you, my dear. I had hoped to find you more amiable. The strength of your blood, it appears, is the antitoxin to this particular spell."

"Let them go," she said, surprised at her own vehemence.

"Tsk, tsk, my dear. Even if the spell did not work on you, I'd think you'd be a little more appreciative of my presence. After all, I'm the only one who knows how to read that interesting little bedtime story of Merlin's. Come back to us and I'll help you solve the riddle."

"You don't actually expect me to come back. You can't be that insane."

Shrugging, the dean pinned her with a cold stare. "Can't blame me for trying. It would be easier on you if you did, but I expected you to decline."

"Then why are you here?" Elli watched as the dean walked around, or more accurately, through the other items in the boxcar as if he were taking a stroll in the park, stopping here and there to look at different crates and sacks, his nonchalant manner giving her chills. *What are you up to? Why aren't you getting to the point?*

"Am I making you nervous, my dear?" he asked, innocently, his brown eyes mischievous. When she didn't answer, he laughed, the sound making her cringe inside despite her stubborn vow to not show fear. "You know very well why I'm here. I'm still waiting for an answer to my question from last night. I want to know about your premonitions. What do the lines mean? Where is Merlin's crystal hidden?"

Her surprise at his knowledge of the crystal must have shown on her face, as he added, "Yes, I know of the crystal. And, more importantly, I know what to do with it once it's found. You would do well to tell me now before I release your friends to destroy themselves. You might not have cared if you died, but I'm quite sure you feel differently about their deaths. If you give me the answer, I'll help you keep them from their destructive paths."

"I'll find a way to stop them without your so-called help," she snapped.

"Don't you dare speak to me in that manner!" he growled, his image flickering in and out with his sudden burst of rage and then re-solidifying as he controlled his temper. "I realize that you've only seen the dark part of our Order, but we can be as good as we are bad. We have a lighter side." The tone of his voice had turned silky smooth and persuasive, making Elli think of how the snake must have sounded to Eve in the Garden of Eden.

"Think of it this way. If you joined us, you would become queen of the entire world. You could have everything you've ever wanted and so much more. A different change of clothes for every hour of the day. Diamonds. Rubies. Pearls. Furs from exotic animals. You would be worshipped from dawn until dusk. If you want to keep your friends, fine. You could give each of them their own mansion with servants to wait on their every need. I'll even promise not to harm Derek for his betrayal. He'll be safe and so will your other friends.

No one will get hurt, I swear. Not a drop of innocent blood will be spilled. Join us and together we will find Merlin's crystal. Merge our powers and you will no longer be hunted. Swear to obey me and you'll want for nothing."

"Are you finished with the commercial?" Elli asked, crossing her arms.

"Hmmm," he said, smiling with delight. "I see my offer has spurred your tongue already. Your answer, my dear?"

"Is no!" she exclaimed, passion making her ignore the way the dean seethed. "I'd rather die than join you."

"Silly, stupid girl!" the dean barked. His image flared brightly, a sickly green aura surrounding it as his voice suddenly grew calm, like the moment before a storm. "Well, if you can't be made to see reason through persuasion, perhaps force will work. When your friends have all killed themselves, and you've nowhere to run, you'll come back. I know you will."

"Don't be so sure about that." Elli glared back despite the sudden chill that was raising the hairs on the back of her neck.

"I am quite sure, child. You see, you won't be able to survive without them. If your powers aren't harnessed by Merlin's crystal within thirteen days, you'll die as the power inside you consumes itself."

"You're lying!" she screamed.

"Read it for yourself." With a flick of his wrists, Elli watched the dean's notebook, which had fallen when Cyn Dal had jumped into the fight, rise from the floor. The pages began to fly by as if the wind had fingers, the flapping suddenly stopping at an entry near the end. It took several moments for Elli to make sense of the heavy scrawl. The car seemed to dip and spin around her as the words began to take hold. Sitting down heavily on a crate, she stared at the notebook. "'*June 27, 2015*,'" the dean quoted, every word piercing Elli's heart. "'*Break through! Though the meaning of Merlin's words still elude me, I've managed to make some headway with a few of the smaller passages. It seems that the child has only a short time to live if Merlin's crystal isn't placed upon her forehead at the appointed hour. It does not stop there. If the child dies, the world will be thrown into an inescapable chaos of dark against light that will destroy the human race in the undercurrent. The child is the key to everything!"*

The dean's words seemed to haunt Elli long after he finished speaking and the notebook had fallen once again to the floor. Her ears rang in the long silence. It was odd how even though she was suddenly faced with her own mortality, she felt only emptiness. All the mixed emotions that had been running through her fizzled out like the carbonation escaping a soda can. Speaking through the strange calm that enveloped her, she asked, "If this is true, why do you still want me to join you? All you'd have to do is wait for the thirteen days to be up and then you'd have what you want."

"Ah, but what good is a world without subjects to rule? Besides, power like yours is a rarity. It must be coveted. Cherished. I don't want to see your death, girl, any more than you do." The sadness in the dean's voice made Elli raise her eyes to meet his. His face looked tired. Worn. The shadows under his eyes had deepened and his hair seemed grayer than before. "That's why you must come back to us before it's too late. If you wait too long, you'll die and so will your friends in the aftermath."

Gesturing towards the still forms of Elli's friends, the dean continued, "If you think this is the worst that can happen to them, you are sadly mistaken. The powers that will awaken once you're dead will dwarf any nightmare you can imagine. It will tear them, and the world, apart. There's no hope unless you join us. You don't have a chance."

Letting her eyes drift from the dean to her friends who still stood motionless around her, Elli felt a wave of doubt wash over her. *What if he's telling the truth?* A memory of she and her friends sitting in the common room invaded her thoughts. Page laughing. Teddy peeking over the top of his history book. Cyn Dal sitting in the bean-bag chair, her hair shining from the glow of her laptop's screen. Branda lounging on the couch in her carefree manner. Justin and his soft gray eyes.

Tears sprang to Elli's eyes and she lowered them to keep the dean from seeing. *I can't let them be destroyed. If I give myself up, they would survive....* As she stared at the floor, she realized that she was looking at Merlin's book which had fallen open when Cyn Dal had jumped up. Through misty eyes, she silently begged for an answer to her confusion. She watched the small slits of sunlight play on the book as the train sped on. To her amazement, each time the light touched the pages, the words seemed to change, almost flicker, and then return to normal when the shadows came again. What came as more of a shock was that she recognized the words on the page. It was the poem she'd had premonitions about when first coming to Clandestine. Shakespeare's Sonnet 65. The words seemed to flash gold in the bars of sunlight that ran across the page, drawing her attention to the last lines.

Or what strong hand can hold his swift foot back?
Or who his spoil of beauty can forbid?
O none, unless this miracle have might,
That in black ink my love may still shine bright.

"There's always a chance," she whispered, feeling the weight of the words settle on her.

"What?" the dean asked, his tone forcing her to look him in the face once again. The weakness he'd shown only moments ago was gone, replaced with disbelief and angst.

"There's always a chance," Elli repeated, her calmness turning to strength. "Go away, Dean. You won't tempt me or persuade me into joining a side that I know is wrong."

The dean's face began to change, growing more and more hideous as his rage took shape. His eyes flashed like cold darkness and his face contorted. A command flew from his mottled lips to someone Elli could not see and within seconds her friends were unlocked from their paralysis, ready to kill each other.

Gathering her powers around her, Elli centered herself and focused all her attention on the image of the dean despite the chaos that once again filled the boxcar. Without thought, words began to fall from her lips. "As the descendent of Merlin, and in his name, I command you to go away!" With a piercing shriek, the hologram of the dean flickered and disappeared in a puff of foul green smoke. A resounding clap of thunder filled the small space, making Elli's ears ring but leaving the strange calm she felt untouched.

Immediately after the sound, Justin's red eyes softened to gray as his sanity returned. Looking down at the fire ball in his hand, he slowly closed his fist to extinguish it. Derek followed his example. "What happened?" he asked.

"I don't know," Branda began, releasing Cyn Dal's hair with a repentant look that was returned with an apology from the fair-skinned girl. "All I remember is being so mad at everyone that I could've –" she paused. Elli could sense the ending of her sentence through the telepathic link.

"I'm so sorry, everyone," Page said, close to tears. Teddy placed a brotherly hand on her shoulder as he apologized as well.

"It isn't your fault," Elli said, giving Page a reassuring smile. "It was the dean. He made you want to destroy each other."

"What!" Cyn Dal exclaimed, exasperated. "How?"

"Bloody hell. Emotional Projection." Derek's voice was full of annoyance as he slammed his fist into the wall and then whipped around to lean his back against it.

"What's that?" Teddy asked, coming to stand behind Cyn Dal.

"It's like astral projection. You focus on a person or a small group of people and you control them through their emotions. You can make them do anything you want when they're beyond thought. Yarrow perfected it since it uses air somehow." The forecast was like a whisper of doom. If the dean could do that, what else could he do?

"How can they be that strong that they can reach us here, on a moving train?" Page asked.

"The Acolytes link up through a blood binding. They slice their hands and then clasp them together in a circle, blood to blood. The more people in the series, the more powerful it is. As to how they actually use the element of air, we students were never privy to. They sometimes used our blood when they wanted to control over great distances, but that's it. I don't really know any more than that. They didn't trust us enough to share their methods."

"And how often did you give your blood willingly?" Justin asked, narrowing his eyes.

"You make it sound like I a choice," Derek replied huskily. "Need I remind you that I was just as affected by the Acolytes' little stunt as you were."

"Small penance for what you've done in the past."

"We can't all be altar boys, Spaller," Derek snapped.

"Will you two knock it off!" Elli exclaimed, breaking in, her temper flaring in annoyance. "We've got more things to worry about than Derek's past." Despite the strength of her words, she gave an involuntary shiver at the anger that still surrounded Justin and Derek. Though the balls of flame had been extinguished, the heat seemed to still remain. The dean's spell had fed their hatred toward each other.

"She's right, you know," Branda said, plopping down on a crate and pulling her legs into a yoga position. "We really should start thinking about some kind of retaliation for whatever they throw at us next."

"You can't plan ahead for this kind of thing," Derek said, running a hand through his hair. "The Acolytes have tools at their disposal that you can't possibly imagine. There is no escaping them."

Sensing the comment that was about to erupt out of Justin, Elli cut him off. "But we just can't sit here. There has to be some way."

"How did you stop the dean this time?" Cyn Dal asked.

"I don't think I did. It was Merlin's book. I can read it."

"What?" six voices chimed in unison.

"It's true. The dean offered me a deal and it was after that I could read the book," Elli paused, picking up the book. She paged through it, trying to recall even the slightest detail, her heart skipping a beat as she thought back to the dean's words. It was then that a sliver of sunlight flickered across the pages, changing the letters from their incomprehensible shape to recognizable words and then back again as the light passed. "It's the sun!" she exclaimed with excitement. "We need to open the door."

Grasping the steel handle, Justin slid the door open, letting more of the sunlight flood the small car. Before Elli's eyes, the words on the page began to transform, revealing the poem once again. Setting it down on a crate, her friends crowded around her, peaking at the pages. Elli smiled with triumph. "See!"

"See what?" Justin asked, peering closely at the volume. "Nothing happened. It still looks the same to me."

"You've got to be kidding!" she replied. Glancing down at the page again, the poem was still there. "You really can't read it?" Elli asked, her voice sounded soft to her own ears in the midst of the clack from the train's wheels. The looks on her friends' faces told her that the words on the page were as incomprehensible as Martian. Setting the book down again, Elli felt the burning sting of frustration rush through her. "I don't understand."

"Maybe we aren't supposed to be able to read it. Only you are. Like what happened with the dean and the box," Page pondered, her chin resting on her fist as she sat cross-legged on a pile of flour sacks.

"I don't buy that," Derek said. "The message in the box was addressed to us, too. Besides, the dean was able to translate some of the smaller parts of the book already. If it was only meant for Elli, he shouldn't have been able to make *any* headway."

"Love," Justin began, his voice strangely cautious as the sunlight played in his hair, "you said that Clandestine offered you a deal. What kind of deal?"

Choosing her words carefully while avoiding his eyes, Elli explained, "He said that if I returned to Clandestine, he'd leave you all alone –"

"Which is something you didn't even consider for a minute, right?" Page interrupted, the certainty on her face only wavering when Elli didn't answer. The silence that followed was strange, like someone shutting off an extremely loud radio that had been playing for hours. There was a kind of pressure in her ears. Out of the corner of her eye, she watched the expression on Justin's face become unreadable. Only the strain in his chiseled jaw gave any evidence of the emotions bubbling under the surface.

"Elli, did you..." Cyn Dal began, her voice trailing off, her almond-shaped eyes worried.

"No, of course not." A feeling of insecurity began to seep into Elli's bones, erasing the last of the calmness that had been there when facing the dean.

"But you thought about it," Derek said, crossing his arms, and giving her a look that made her flush. Afraid to speak, Elli nodded.

"Don't you ever do about that again!" Justin suddenly shouted, clearing the distance between them in a single step, his gray eyes snapping as he faced her. "I don't want you to even consider selling yourself to them. I don't care if they're holding a bloody gun to my head. You walk away! Do you understand?" He turned away to move toward the door, putting distance again between them. "How could you even consider it?" he added, turning back toward her.

"What did you expect her to do, Spaller?" Derek broke in. "She wasn't just trying to save our lives, but this rotten world as well. You know as well as I do that if this little army goes poof, there won't be anyone left to fight the dean."

"Would you want her blood on your hands, Derek?" Branda asked, her blue eyes sparkling and her tattoo standing out starkly against her pale skin. "I know I wouldn't. I wouldn't want her to give herself up to save my backside.

Besides, if she's alive, there's still a chance."

Elli could feel a silent agreement emanating from the others through the telepathic web as they looked at her. Suddenly unable to hold their gazes, she let her eyes drift back to the open pages of the book. It appeared that a small spot of gold colored light had formed at the center of the book, resting in the crevice between the flapping pages.

"Look," she said, pointing. Before their eyes, the spot began to grow, changing from an indescribable shape to a golden lotus about the size of Elli's palm. The flower shimmered in the sunlight as it began to change shape again, becoming a flame that flickered as it rose from the pages. It then transformed into a small white cloud with a golden lining. Watching it intently, Elli felt a rush of awe as it began to spread out over their heads, becoming a fluffy blanket that covered the ceiling of the boxcar. Feeling something touch her cheek, she lifted her hand to wipe it away, realizing that it was a drop of moisture that had begun to trickle down her skin like a single tear.

Before she had a chance to be surprised, the rain began. It came in a fine drizzle of rainbow colors that twinkled in the sunlight like tiny jewels. Blues. Indigos. Reds. Greens. Colors Elli couldn't describe. They soaked her clothes without staining. They dripped from her hair. Reaching out her hand to catch the drops falling around her, she felt a strong hand entwine with hers. Turning, she found Justin smiling at her, his animosity washed away by the strange rain. A smile seemed to spread around the group as they let the water fall on them, letting it soak in and wash away the last traces of the dean's handiwork.

As lightning flickered, Elli saw images appear on the whiteness of the cloud, like movies projected on to it, the pictures changing with every flash. There was the train surrou-ndded by rolling hills of emerald-green vegetation. A ship floating on a writhing sea of wind-tossed waves. Red flames surrounding a purple stone.

"The book!" Cyn Dal cried, drawing everyone's gaze from the flashing pictures above their heads to the ancient volume. As Cyn Dal reached to cover it, fearing it would be ruined by the water, Teddy placed a hand on her shoulder, making the girl stop.

"Look what's happening," he said, his Southern accent strong. Stepping toward the book, Elli and the others watched as the multi-colored rain began to wash the dark pen strokes away, revealing gold-colored letters beneath – the same letters she'd seen before. It was only when the page was completely free that the rain began to disperse. Glancing up, Elli saw a thin ribbon of rainbow-colored light emerge from inside the cloud and wrap around the fluffy mass, drawing it into itself. In a matter of breaths, it was gone, disappearing in the sunlight, leaving the rain-soaked seven and their newly awakened spell book in silence.

Chapter 9

"That's the answer to Merlin's riddle," Page said, pulling the last of the now-dried articles from the homemade clothes line Teddy and Derek had strung up to dry their drenched clothing. Looking up from the bag she was packing, Elli gave Page a puzzled look. Though they had long closed the door to keep prying eyes from seeing them, the last rays of red-orange sunlight still rained through the slats in the car walls, making designs on the piles of repacked foodstuff.

"What are you talking about?" Branda asked, handing a box of canned corn to Justin for re-stacking.

"Merlin said that the book can only be read when brilliance and selflessness light the way. The brilliance was sunlight and the selflessness was our reaction toward Elli's willingness to give herself up to save our lives. Rather ingenious if I do say so. Merlin knew that the Acolytes could never show that kind of courage."

"Too bad that the dean's notebook didn't make it through the rain," Justin said, picking up the sodden volume from the floor and paging through it. "Almost all the writing has been washed away. It might have held some answers for us."

"We'll just have to make do without it," Elli replied,

shivering to herself at what secrets his journal held. Deep down she was glad that it had been destroyed. Her friends could never discover the truth about the time limit if it was gone. "And we *will* make out just fine."

"She's right, you know," Cyn Dal added, peeking over the cover of Merlin's history. While the others had been busy putting the boxcar back in order after the magical storm, she had crawled into a corner to read the newly uncovered pages. To their amazement, the words had still remained legible even in the shadows. The enchantment surrounding it had been washed away by the rain. "I think in the end all we need is Merlin's book."

"Well, now that we can read it, what does it say?" Derek asked, lazily stretching out on a pile of sacks he'd just finished piling up.

"You don't expect her to read a book that thick in only a few hours, do you?" Teddy chimed in, taking the clothes line down and winding it up.

"No. I just thought she might be able to tell us a little bit about what we're headed for. After all, no one has any information on the crystal. It could be a decoy."

"I don't think Merlin would send us after it if it wasn't important," Elli replied. "Besides, didn't you see the images in the cloud? I'd like to think the book is kind of like a road map for us since we don't have a clue where we're going. All we have is a direction. West."

"So far, Elli's right. The book is kind of like a treasure map. Look." Pulling a crate closer, Cyn Dal placed the book on top, the cover making a pleasant rustling sound as it scraped across the slats.

Sitting next to Cyn Dal, Elli peered at the pages. Scrawled across the paper was a topographical map. Running her hand across the page, Elli could feel the roughness of the paper mixed with the uneven texture of three-dimensional hills and rivers.

"Okay. This is us," Cyn Dal said, pointing at a small glowing spot that reminded Elli of a "You are here" locator dot on a mall directory. The dot was moving slowly across the page toward a large mass of blue tinted paper off to the left.

"Elli's premonitions and the cloud told us that we should look for Merlin's crystal at sea. We're almost there," Justin said, looking over Cyn Dal's shoulder. "At the rate we're going, we should be there tomorrow morning."

"That's great, but what do we do then? Even if we hijack a boat it isn't like we have much of a chance finding the talisman. The ocean isn't a bathtub," Derek said, breaking in.

"You *always* look at the bright side, don't you," Branda replied sarcastically, shaking her head.

"Don't worry, Blackwell. If I have my way, we'll be leaving you at the pier, so you won't have to wonder about things like that," Justin said, crossing his arms, a smile twitching at the corner of his mouth.

"None of us has to worry," Cyn Dal interrupted, stopping Derek before he could comment. "Watch." Picking up the book, Cyn Dal turned her body, facing north. As she moved, the light on the page dimmed and then finally disappeared, reappearing only when she was facing west again. "We have a guide," she explained, smiling.

***

The moon shining through the slats of the boxcar gave the stacks of foodstuff an eerie glow as Elli lay in her flour sack nest, her back to Justin. Letting her eyes wander around the room, she tried to ignore the reason she wasn't able to sleep. Every time she closed her eyes, she could almost hear the loud ticking of a clock as it counted down the remaining minutes of her life. It was better just to stay awake until exhaustion took her. It was better to not think about how little time she had left.

A soft fluttering noise drew her eyes to the door. Her nightmare from last night invading her mind, Elli felt her heart quicken as she tried to swallow the lump that had suddenly taken up residence in her throat. She peered into the darkness, afraid to stir, a reaction left over from childhood – when you were safe as long as you didn't move. To her surprise, she found a dark pair of eyes twinkling in the moonlight and the soft smell of apple wood tickling her nose. Sighing with relief, feeling her building adrenaline dissipate, she slowly crawled from her bed so as to not wake Justin.

Taking Derek's outstretched hand, Elli let him lead her toward a corner of the car where a stack of crates hid them from view.

"What's up?" she asked, sitting on a box in the moonlit corner, her jeans making a scraping noise on the wooden slats as she sat down.

"I just thought you'd like to talk." Even though he was perched on a crate across from her, his arms crossed, leaning back lazily against the wall, Derek screamed alertness, his senses taking in the room around him, as if he were waiting for something. Though it was hard to see his features in the darkness, only half his face lit by the dim light, it didn't matter. He was still handsome, his full lips in a half-playful, half-secretive smile. Ignoring the slight flutter in her chest at the look in his eyes, Elli sighed again.

"Talk about what?"

"You know very well what I'm referring to."

"Derek, I'm not really in the mood for games –"

"I'm not playing one!" he hissed, reaching for her from the shadows, his hands wrapping around her arms and pulling her toward him. The anxiety he kept hidden under a thick blanket of conceit was now plain in the moonlight, bare and raw like scraped skin. It was then that she *did* know what he was talking about. In that moment of weakness, she had an almost irresistible urge to fall into his arms and cry the tears she'd been holding back ever since the dean had told her.

Instead Elli looked down, trying desperately to disregard the tingles his hands were sending up the bare skin of her arms. "How long have you known?" Her voice was quiet even to her own ears.

She felt a tender hand under her chin as he raised her eyes

to his. "You forget who I am. Who I was," he said, softly. As if he was unaware of how his touch was making her traitorous body react, he slowly let his hands slide down her arms, finally taking her hands in his. Though her first impulse was to pull her hands away, Elli saw the agonized pain and remorse in Derek's eyes and couldn't find it in her heart to let go.

"I was the dean's trusted apprentice and confidant. I saw things that..." Elli heard the apprehension in his voice and gently squeezed his hands to reassure him that she understood. After a moment, he continued, "Well, let's just say that I saw things. And heard them. That's how I found out about the time limit. I know that we only have a few days until you...."

"Die," she said, the sound of the word almost bringing it closer. A shudder ran up her spine, making her shiver in the damp night air. Without a word, Derek unbuttoned his over-shirt, one he'd borrowed from Justin's bag, and placed it around her shoulders, the scent of smoked apple wood wafting over her. The lingering body heat on the soft, blue cotton was welcome and helped soothe the chills running up her arms. "Won't you be cold?"

"Warm-blooded," he said, giving her a tender smile that made her heart flip strangely. A silence fell over them in the darkness. The only sound was the staccato sounds of the train running over the iron tracks. In the quiet, Elli could feel him appraising her – the shape of her face, the curve of her mouth, her dark hair cascading in waves over her shoulders. The sensation made her feel uncomfortable and yet strangely beautiful at the same time. Even thoughts of Justin didn't stop how Derek's soft look almost felt like a physical caress on her cheek.

Knowing that she had to break the silence somehow, Elli spoke, her voice surprisingly steady, "Are you going to tell the others?"

"Do you want me to?"

"No. They have enough to worry about with the dean breathing down our necks. I don't want them to have one more thing to be concerned with."

"You mean you don't want Justin to worry, don't you."

It wasn't a question, but Elli nodded anyway, feeling her chest tighten as a wave of hopelessness hit her. "In the end," she paused, feeling tears begin to sting her eyes. "Promise me, Derek. Promise me you'll take care of him. Of all of them. If anything should happen –"

"That's enough!" he said, his voice low but filled with anguish as he once again pulled her to him, wrapping his arms around her as if holding on would keep the truth at bay. "I swear that nothing bad will happen to you. I'll keep you safe even if you don't lo – even if you don't think there's any hope. Trust me." Derek's voice dripped with a mixture of emotions as Elli found herself holding him back out of fear and pain, tears streaming down her cheeks. "I promise that I'll take care of you," he said, pulling back just enough to look into her face, his eyes dark with determination as he wiped her tears away. "And then," he began, holding her in his arms as if she were a child, running his fingers through her hair, "I'll take care of them."

Chapter 10

"Wake up, everybody! Wake up!" an anxious voice yelled, waking Elli with a start. Sitting up, she found Derek half-hanging out of the door as he called again. "Come on, you guys. Get up! We've got problems."

"What's wrong?" Justin asked, springing from his place beside Elli, his hair still ruffled from sleep.

"The bloody train is turning!"

"What?" Branda and Justin exclaimed in unison as they rushed to look out. The smell of the ocean wafted into the box. Looking outside, Elli saw the sea before her, dark and vast under a slate-gray sky. As the train crowned a hill, she saw the track off in the distance. It ran parallel with the shore and then turned to the south, away from the water, until it disappeared behind some distant hills. Wherever this train was going, it was not stopping at some ocean-side station like she'd hoped.

Leaning back, she saw that Justin and Branda had also had the same realization, grim looks appearing on their faces.

"Maybe we're supposed to turn with the train," Cyn Dal said, pulling Merlin's book into her lap and letting it open to the map. Shifting the book, she was disappointed to see that the marking that represented them disappeared when she moved the book in the direction the tracks were going.

"So, what's the verdict?" Page asked.

"We have to get off," Cyn Dal replied, closing the book with a loud snap.

"Correction. We have to jump," Branda added.

"Great!" Page replied, sarcastically.

"We should pack some of this food up and take it with us," Teddy said, opening his bag and tossing some apples into it. "We don't have a lot of money and renting a boat is going to be expensive."

"That's a good idea though I think we should leave the owner some kind of compensation for it," Justin added, putting some cans in his pack.

"Why? You just heard what Teddy said. We don't have a lot of money," Derek replied.

"I don't know what you're used to, Blackwell, but we don't steal," Justin snapped, meeting the boy's dark eyes.

"You didn't seem to mind filling your gob yesterday without asking. Why change your tune now?" Derek's eyes were taunting, his lips curled in a sneer.

"Come on, guys. It's too early in the morning for this," Cyn Dal broke in, punctuating her comment by digging into her pockets for some wadded-up bills. "I think Justin's right. We should leave something for the owner."

"Glad that's settled," Page mumbled just low enough for Elli to hear as they finished packing the last of their belongings and some foodstuffs in their bags. "But at least it will all be over soon."

"What do you mean?" Elli whispered back.

"After we leave Derek behind, maybe Justin will stop being so jumpy then."

Elli sat back on her heels. Despite both Justin and Branda's comments, she hadn't really thought about leaving Derek behind and after last night, she knew she couldn't. He had to take care of her friends if the prophesy... when the prophesy came true. Besides, if she did die, Derek could help

Justin and the others against the Acolytes. His fire power would come in handy. *But what about Justin? Shouldn't you tell him about the time limit,* a little voice called in the back of her mind. Chewing her lip, Elli busily finished her packing in an effort to avoid answering the question. *I can't tell him. He'll tie me up, throw me over his shoulder, and not stop running until he reaches Iceland. I know he means well, and I almost wish he'd do it, but I can't save the world that way.* Elli snorted at the comedy of it all. After all, how often does a girl get to say she's going to save the world and really mean it?

"What's so funny?" Page asked.

"Nothing. Page, do you think that we should really leave Derek behind?"

"Sure. Don't you?"

"I don't know. He might come in handy. I mean, he –"

"Elli, he can't come with us," Page interrupted, placing a hand on her friend's arm. "I know you feel some kind of responsibility toward him since he saved your life –"

"Twice."

"Twice. But I don't know if we should trust him with Merlin's crystal. It's just too important."

"Come on, you guys. We've got to go!" Branda called, a wild grin on her face as she stood in the open door. Picking up their bags, Elli and the others made their way over to the door. Page and Elli's conversation was lost in the noise of the clicking track beneath them as the grass whipped by in a green blur. "We don't want to miss our stop!" Branda added with a laugh.

"That's what I'm afraid of!" Page hollered back.

"What?"

"The sudden stop!"

"You should throw your bag out and then jump," Justin yelled to be heard over the wind. "Roll when you hit the ground!"

"Sounds like you've done this before, Spaller. I always knew you were part hobo," Derek laughed mockingly.

Narrowing his eyes at Derek for a split second, Justin

turned his attention back to the scenery that whipped by. "I'll go first. Don't forget to roll." Taking Elli's hand in his, he quickly kissed the back of her hand, gave her a wink, threw his bag out and then jumped. Leaning out the door, Elli saw him roll to a stop and then stand up.

"Okay, Branda, you're next!" Derek yelled over the din. With a loud whoop, Branda launched himself out the door. One by one they jumped until only Elli and Derek were left. "Go on, Lady Allison! Your turn."

Steeling herself, Elli walked to the edge and looked down. The sight of the ground whipping by under her made her eyes swim dizzily.

"What's wrong? You've gotta jump! We can't let the others get too far away!"

"Sorry! It's just a little vertigo," Elli exclaimed, her heart beating loudly in her ears as her stomach tightened.

"Listen, if you're too scared –," he ridiculed.

"I'm not scared!" she interrupted as his tone angered her. Throwing her bag out the door, Elli took a deep breath and leapt. The ground seemed to rush up to meet her, knocking the wind out of her as she rolled to a stop. Lying in the grass, she stared up at the gray clouds overhead as she breathed slowly in and out, trying to calm her racing heart. She heard a *thump* next to her as Derek landed only a few feet away. Sitting up, she watched the train fade into the distance, it's clacking noise carried away on the wind. The sudden silence was strange after two days of the rhythmic sound of the metal wheels on the spurs.

Elli watched Derek pull himself to his feet and make his way over to her. Taking the hand that he offered, he helped her up. She ignored the way his hand held hers for a breath too long before she pulled away, focusing on wiping the grass and dirt from her jeans. Looking up, she caught his smile.

"What are you smiling at?" she asked.

"I knew that would get you to jump. You really should watch that temper of yours, though," he smirked.

Ignoring the urge to hit him, Elli glared defiantly into his dark eyes. "Look who's talking about tempers." Her remark only made his smile broaden. She couldn't help herself. Even though she tried hard to stay mad at him, Elli couldn't fight the smile that spread across her face. "You're impossible," she said, throwing her hands up in the air.

"That's what I've been told," he replied, picking her pack up and placing it on his shoulder. The sound of crunching gravel made them turn. "Looks like the cavalry has arrived."

"Are you two all right?" Cyn Dal asked, running up along the stony spur. "What took you so long to jump?"

"I had a little vertigo," Derek said, making Elli stare at him in surprise. "Elli had to talk me into jumping."

"And I thought you were fearless, Blackwell," Justin taunted, getting revenge for the hobo comment made earlier on the train.

"I need to have some faults to balance out my perfections. Otherwise I'd be too good to live with," he replied, not rising to Justin's remark.

"Obviously modesty isn't a bloody problem for you, then," Branda retorted.

"I think we should keep going," Cyn Dal said, breaking in. "We've still got a few miles to walk until we reach the shore." Pulling out Merlin's book, she opened it to the map. A bright dot of light flashed where they stood, pointing ever west. In silence they started off, following the track for a short while. Where it turned off to the south, they continued on west, Justin and Branda leading the way, lost in conversation, Derek, Cyn Dal, Teddy and finally Elli following.

After they had been walking for a while, Elli noticed Derek dropping back slowly until he was walking beside her. Keeping his voice low, he said, "I'm sure you're wondering why I told the others what I did." Taking her silence as a 'yes,' he continued, "If Justin knew you were scared of jumping off the train, he probably would have used it against you."

"How so?"

"You know as well as I do that he's looking for any excuse he can to get you to change your mind about fighting in this war. I can't say that I blame him. I don't want to see you hurt either, but I know that running away is the last thing you should do. You've only got twelve more days left. He's so thick-headed that he'd probably have you bloody well packed off before you could even explain."

"Thanks," she whispered back after several moments of thinking over what he'd said, and they fell once again into silence. Elli's thoughts weighed heavily on what she would do when it came time for her and the others to continue their quest across the sea. She knew in her soul that Derek had to come with them. It was a feeling that she couldn't explain, but it would be hard to convince the others on that alone. Their current tolerance of him would only last so long. She realized how hard it was on Justin to have his enemy there, constantly needling him, but Elli just couldn't bring herself to believe that Derek was all bad. He'd helped her today. She'd looked into his eyes last night. He might be harsh and chauvinistic sometimes, but he always seemed to come through. They needed that whether Justin and the others wanted to admit it or not.

"What's the matter, Lady Allison?" Derek asked quietly, breaking the silence again.

"Just thinking," she replied in the same, soft tone.

"I see." He was quiet for a moment. "You don't trust me, do you?"

"I wouldn't have asked you to watch over my friends if I didn't."

"Then why won't you tell me what's going on behind those pretty eyes of yours?" he questioned, looking at her meaningfully.

Sighing, she ran a hand through her hair. "The others don't want you to come with us to find Merlin's crystal. They want to leave you behind."

"What do you want?" he asked, his voice barely audible.

"I don't know what I want," she whispered back with exasperation. "I have this feeling that you should come with us, but what if…."

"What if they're right and you're wrong," he finished for her. She could feel the hurt he tried to hide behind his nonchalant tone, and it made her feel cold inside.

"Derek, I'm sorry," she said sadly. "But what if you're still connected to the dean and don't know it? You've proven yourself to me again and again, and I can't help but trust you after everything you've done, but I don't trust where you came from."

"Elli, just tell me what you want. Whatever it is, I'll do it. I swear." Derek's voice, though he kept it soft, had a finality to it that tugged at her heart. Looking ahead, Elli saw the brave group walking along before her, and she felt a warming sensation in her chest as she looked at her friends. Her family. They had welcomed her without hesitation and had vowed to help her succeed no matter the cost. *No matter the cost*, she said silently to herself.

Turning, she looked into Derek's eyes for the span on several heartbeats before she said, "You're coming with us. Even though I know they aren't going to like it. I – they need you."

"So be it," he whispered.

"But how are we going to get them to let you come with us?"

"Leave it all to me, Lady Allison. I have a plan."

***

After a few hours of walking, the sound of the ocean filled Elli's ears as she and her friends topped an embankment. Below them was sprawled a rocky beach with water lapping at the shore. Elli couldn't help but smile and feel that they'd accomplished a huge feat by getting this far. "We made it!" she said, unable to keep the excitement from her voice.

"We haven't made anything, yet," Justin replied, his gray eyes scanning the beach.

"Ever the optimist," she laughed, refusing to let him dampen her spirits. Taking his hand in hers, she gave it a playful squeeze, receiving a small smile in return as he raised her hand to his lips and gently kissed it.

"*That's because you bring the best out in me,*" he said to her, his mental voice warm in her mind.

"Hey! Look!" Page exclaimed, pointing to the south-west. Turning, Elli saw a fishing village tucked between a hillside and a sheer cliff, less than two miles away. Boats and small fishing trawlers were moored in a tiny harbor and smoke billowed from the chimneys of small establishments which lined the town's roads.

"Now that's what I call luck," Elli said as she began making her way toward the village, Justin and her friends in tow.

The sun was beginning to get low in the sky by the time they reached the town. The mingled scents of fish, saltwater and baking bread wafted over them. As they wandered the streets, they received some strange looks from the locals. Looking down, Elli realized what she and her friends must look like. Even though Merlin's magical rainwater had washed the worst of the dust of Clandestine from their skins, the combination of sleeping in a boxcar and a long trek across the countryside had left them bedraggled and dirty once again. Deciding that the best place to start was the harbor, Elli and her friends made their way toward it, trying their best not to drool at the enticing smells wafting from the open kitchen windows of the town inn.

Only a few fishermen were found on the docks. Most, it appeared, had already gone home to supper.

"Excuse me, sir," Elli said as they walked up to a friendly-looking old man who was busily mending a net.

Taking his pipe from his mouth, revealing several missing teeth that lead to a few gaps in his smile, the man eyed them kindly from the crate he was sitting on. "'Ow can I 'elp you, lass?"

"Do you know where we could borrow or rent a boat around here?" Justin asked.

"That's 'ard to say, lad. 'Tis the busy season. Most of us

earn a livin' with our boats 'n a few days withouta catch means the difference between payin' the mortgage and lettin' our young'uns starve."

"We'd be happy to pay for it," Elli added.

"That may be so, but 'less you can also pay for the lost fish, 'n' at market prices, I'll wager you're goin' to be 'ard pressed to find someone."

"We don't have a lot of money," Page said, sadly.

"Sorry I am to 'ear that."

"What if we had the money?" Derek asked, breaking in, receiving a glare from Justin.

"Well, lad, if you 'ad the money, then I'd suggest talking to young Tom O'Riley, cap'n of the *Lois Jane*. She's second to last on the far dock there."

"Thanks," Elli said, giving him a smile as she and the others went in search of the *Lois Jane*. Giving her a nod, he went back to his net mending, a smoke ring encircling his head as he puffed on his pipe.

"What do you mean if we had the money?" Justin hissed. "You know bloody well we have less than a hundred pounds. That isn't going to make up for however long this Tom O'Riley is going to miss fishing."

"You worry too much, Spaller. Just go with the flow," Derek replied nonchalantly, oblivious to Justin's seething.

"I hate to add fuel to the fire, but Justin's right," Teddy said. "Where are we going to get the money to pay him?"

"I have it all under control," Derek said.

"Under control!" Justin exclaimed, stopping dead in his tracks. "What do you mean 'under control'?"

However, before Derek could respond, Branda, who had walked ahead of the group, called back. "There's the *Lois Jane*!" she exclaimed, pointing toward a small fishing trawler.

As they neared the boat, Elli felt a slight twinge of apprehension at the condition of it. The blue painted sides were chipped and a line of rust ran between the words *Lois* and *Jane* on the back. The helm was encased in a small room with large windows and an open door that hung awkwardly on its hinges. Through the opening, Elli could see a kind of trap door that must have gone below deck. The deck, itself, must have been painted white at one time, but it looked as though it had seen better days. Netting and rope were piled haphazardly in one corner. Elli saw two old tires, tied with fraying nylon rope, slung over the sides to keep the boat from smashing into the dock. Below the tires, she could see the white tops of barnacles which clung to the underbelly of the boat.

"I don't know about you guys," Branda began as the sound of someone tinkering with an engine reached them, "but the idea of swimming sounds better and better to me." In agreement, they began to walk away from the *Lois Jane.* It was only the sound of barking that made Elli pause. Turning, she saw a dog, about the size of a collie, bounding toward them from somewhere on ship. It put its front paws on the rail and continued to bark until even the others stopped and turned. An odd chill of recognition echoed through Elli's mind. She'd seen this dog before. His light brown coat. His dark brown and very floppy ears. He was the barking dog from her premonition.

"Toby, quiet!" a voice yelled from the ship. When the dog, Toby, continued, a young man, probably in his early thirties, stepped out from the open door of the helm, wiping his greasy hands on an even greasier rag, his red hair combed back from his forehead.

"Don't mind him," the man said, silencing the dog with a look. Toby, his tail wagging and his tongue hanging happily from his mouth, pulled his paws from the rail and sat beside the man. "He just gets over-excited when we have visitors."

"We didn't mean to bother you," Justin said. "Are you Tom O'Riley?"

"That'd be me."

"We were told that you might be interested in renting out your boat to us," Branda explained.

"And who told you that, lass?"

"An older man over there," Page said, gesturing toward where the man had been.

"Did he smoke a pipe and have a bit of a cockney accent?"

"Yes," she replied.

"Then that would be old Edward Joseph. He has a knack for pointing people in the right direction," Tom began, rubbing the back of his hand on his forehead, leaving a trail of grease just above his brow, "even when they don't want to go."

"Then you'll rent your boat to us?" Page asked, a broad smile spreading over her pixie-like face.

"That depends on two things. The first is on where you're going and the second is on how long you plan on being gone."

"We're not sure how long we'll be gone. It won't be more than a few days out though," Elli said, adding a silent, *I hope*.

"Mr. Joseph didn't mention how much you would charge for the boat," Justin said, trying to avoid the question of where they were going. The less Tom O'Riley knew, the better for all of them.

"Considering how long I'd miss out on fishing, three hundred pounds would seem fair."

"But we only –"

"It's a deal," Derek said, cutting Cyn Dal off.

Whirling to look at him, Elli couldn't keep the shock from her face. Derek met her gaze

"What are you talking about? We don't have three hundred pounds!" Justin hissed.

"Can you give us a second?" Teddy asked, looking at Tom. Receiving a nod of approval, they moved to the end of the dock out of earshot.

"What do you mean it's a deal? We don't have that kind of money," Branda said, crossing her arms and cocking her head in such a way that the eyes of her dragon and phoenix tattoo looked piercing.

"I have it. What choice do we have but to pay the man what he asks?"

"We? We! There is no bloody *we*. There's *you* and then

there's *us*, and *you* are staying here while the rest of *us* are moving on. End of discussion," Justin snarled.

"Come on, guys!" Page said, breaking in, frustrated. "I think we're missing the bigger picture. I don't know if I want to trust my life to that rust-bucket back there."

"Edward Joseph said that no one else would rent, remember? It's either this or we all get very wet," Teddy explained.

"But that doesn't solve the money problem," Cyn Dal said, tucking a piece of her long, straight, dark hair behind her ear.

"I said I'll take care of it," Derek replied.

"In exchange for a seat, right?" Justin snapped.

"I go where my money goes. If you don't like it, take a bloody canoe. As for me, I'm renting that boat and helping Elli get where she needs to go. You can either tag along or sit here and feed the sea gulls." Derek's voice was cold like chipped ice. Elli could feel the rage in Justin as his eyes began to turn a smoky-red color and his jaw tightened as he ground his teeth with resentment. Everything seemed to go silent as the world waited for one of them to lunge at the other.

A wetness and the feel of a rough tongue on her hand made Elli look down to find Toby staring up at her, a whine escaping him as he stared at her with his large, brown eyes. Her premonition tickled at her mind. She knew that they had to go with Tom O'Riley and Toby. There was no choice.

"We take the *Lois Jane*," Elli said, speaking for the first time. Her voice sounded odd to her ears as she began to pet the top of Toby's head, his soft fur like silk under her fingers.

"What?" Justin asked incredulously, shifting his eyes just slightly to look at her, but not enough to look like he was backing down.

With Toby still at her side, Elli put her hand gently on Justin's arm. "I said we're taking the *Lois Jane*."

"But love, we can't afford it," he said, exasperated.

"Derek said he was going to pay, so it's settled. We're going. All of us."

"*No, love,*" he began, his telepathic voice stern, "*I am not budging on this. Blackwell stays here. I am not trusting your life or Merlin's crystal to him.*"

"*You're going to have to. There's no other way.*" Before he could say anything else or act on the impulsive emotions that she could feel through their link, the ones that told him to throw her over his shoulder and head back to Ravenwood, Elli walked to the *Lois Jane* with Toby in tow and said, "We'll take her."

"Excellent. I have a little work to do in preparation, so I'll see you bright and early tomorrow morning. We leave with the tide."

"We?"

"You don't expect me to let you take my boat out without me, did you?" Before Elli could answer, Tom went on. "You should buy some supplies for the trip. Canned goods, fresh fruit, and such should be fine. You can find them at McGee's Grocery up the street. There should be room at the inn if you need a place to stay." With a whistle to Toby who licked Elli's hand before jumping aboard, Tom disappeared back into the boat, leaving Elli and the others standing on the dock in the setting sun.

Chapter 11

The hot water seeped into the Elli's bones as she leaned her head back on the lip of the old cast-iron tub, the grime of her travels washed away, leaving her skin and hair clean with the scent of soap wafting around her in the steam from the bath. The proprietor of the inn had been ecstatic that she and the others had wanted to rent a room for the night. Apparently, the village saw few visitors, and the inn did most of its business selling meals in the large dining room downstairs. He had let them have two rooms for a very reasonable price and had even taken their very dirty clothes to clean them. Elli had purposefully waited for the others to shower, change and leave for supplies before she took her turn in their shared bathroom. She wanted to relax and let the water unlock the tensions stored inside her.

Closing her eyes, she let her mind wander. She thought of Marion and what she was doing alone in Ravenwood. She thought of her Great-Uncle Ambrose and wondered if he even missed her. *Hardly*, she smirked mentally. But most of all she thought about what lay before her and the others. Elli felt her hands begin to tingle and her pulse quicken as a premonition invaded her mind, forcing her to grip the sides of the tub.

A storm. Blue lightning. Justin and Derek. Shaking hands as they held fireballs aimed at each other. The *Lois Jane* bobbing like a bath toy in a storm. *O fearful meditation! where alack... shall Time's best jewel from Time's chest lie hid... Or what strong hand can hold his swift foot back?*

Opening her eyes, Elli flinched at the brightness of the bathroom light. The water surrounding her no longer felt warm and inviting but cold and oppressive. Getting out of the tub, she dried herself off and brushed her hair while she thought about her latest vision. The sight of Justin and Derek fighting gave her a little twinge of guilt. Elli knew that she had put Derek between herself and Justin on the dock. It was quite apparent that Justin was aware of it too as he hadn't spoken to, or even looked at, her since. When she'd tried to talk to him telepathically later, her efforts were rewarded with a heated silence. She'd thought it best to wait until he came to her.

After Elli dressed in some extra clothes she'd packed in her backpack, she went back out into the bedroom, drawing up short when she saw Justin sitting on the edge of one of the beds, his forearms on his knees and his hands together with his fingers intertwined. Elli had to resist the urge to wince at the glint in his gray eyes.

"I thought you went with the others," she said, keeping her voice level.

"I think we should talk." Elli tried to gage Justin's mood, but it was a strange mixture of anger, pain and... *confusion?* Leaning against the wall, she waited for him to continue. She owed him the first "punch" after what she did on the dock – even if it was for his own good. Justin pinned her with an unwavering look and said, "Elli, what are you up to?"

Right to the point as usual, she thought, finding none of her usual humor. "What do you mean?"

Getting up from the bed, he came to face her, crossing his arms over his chest. "You know bloody well what I mean. Why did you insist that Blackwell come with us? And don't give me any of that we-needed-his-money crap. There's more to it than that. I know it."

"Justin, we need him," she replied, trying to keep her voice calm.

"You mean you need him," he corrected for her flatly, his gray eyes dull.

"What?" Elli felt a kind of chill creeping up her spine.

"I know you better than you think. I've seen the secret looks you give each other. I know there's more going on here. What aren't you telling me?"

"Look," she began, her voice quiet, "I do need Derek to go with us, but it's for a reason that I can't explain to you right now. You have no idea how hard it is for me to say that to you."

"Then why do it?" he asked, his face all edges and angles in the light.

Reaching out her hands, she laid them gently on his crossed arms, willing him to understand. Justin remained rigid and immobile, all except his eyes which flashed with anxiety transformed into indignation. "You have nothing to worry about. I need you to trust me on this and accept that Derek has to go with us —"

Justin dropped his arms and grabbed hers so quickly that Elli's words were lost in her throat. "You can't save him, Elli! I know you want to, but you can't erase someone's past for them! You can't undo the damage they've done!" Justin's words hit her like stones, one by one, making her flinch. He let go of her and walked to the other side of the room, keeping his back to her.

In the unbearable silence that followed his outburst, Elli let the full weight of his words sink in. Even though she hadn't realized that was what she was really trying to do, she knew that she *did* want to save Derek. How could she not? He'd protected her and had kept her secret from the others. She'd looked into his eyes and saw a torment that she wanted to blot out — to give him a chance to redeem himself.

"You're right," she said softly, moving toward Justin's tense form and putting her arms around him, pressing her cheek to his back when he refused to turn toward her embrace. "I do want to save him. I can't help it. How can I be this so-called 'Chosen One' and save the world if I can't even help Derek?" She could hear the touch of sorrow in her own voice.

With a jerk, he broke from her hold and turned to face her, his eyes snapping with hidden fire. "But he isn't worth saving!" he shouted, exasperated as he ran his hands through his hair in frustration. "He's no bloody good. All Blackwell cares about is himself and that's all he'll ever care about. Lies and betrayal are all he knows." Even without their telepathic link, Elli could tell that Justin was holding something back from her, something that reached into the very pit of this blind anger. It tickled at the back of her mind, bringing her premonition back to the surface – Justin and Derek shaking hands while threatening to destroy each other.

"What happened between you and Derek?" she asked, keeping her voice a whisper.

"That's nothing that concerns you!" he seethed, balling his hands into fists at his sides. Even though it took all her composure not to grow angry at this eruption, Elli steeled herself and reached her hand out to cup his cheek, sure that he would recoil at her touch. When he didn't, she let her hand run down his shoulder until, after loosening one finger at a time, she took his hand in hers. Raising it to her own cheek, she heard him mumble something about her playing dirty and it not being fair.

"What is, my love?" she asked, smiling secretly to herself. Elli knew that she could have joined with his mind and taken the information she wanted, but that would have done more harm than good. Instead, she waited patiently for him to lower his walls and to tell her what he kept hidden.

After several moments, Justin took his hand from hers and walked to the window. Looking out, he said roughly, "Are you sure you want to know?"

"I wouldn't have asked if I didn't." Taking a seat on the edge of the bed closest to him, she waited.

In the reflection of the glass pane, Elli could see Justin's eyes go dull as he began to speak. "When I was a kid, I lived in London. My parents somehow scraped up enough money to send me to a private school. It wasn't anything grand like Clandestine University, but it wasn't bad except for the other kids. They were spoiled and snobbish, and as you can guess they didn't really approve of a poor kid with worn-out pants and a faded jacket. My first year there was pretty rough, and I got into a lot of fights. I can remember washing blood from my shirt collar in the basement wash tub so Mum wouldn't see it.

"All that stopped the day that I met Derek Blackwell. I was surrounded by a group of bullies, four to one. Blackwell stepped in to help me even the odds. We both still got pretty banged about, but we became instant friends after it. We did everything together. His parents were rich, but that didn't matter. We hung out for pretty much all of primary school. We even went through the burning together."

"The burning?" Elli questioned.

Without turning to look at her, Justin explained that when an elemental comes into his powers, he has to suffer through them for three days. "Fire elementals tend to have a scorching high fever at a temperature that would kill most people. Earth elementals feel stretched and pulled like how plants feel when they're growing. Air elementals suffer vertigo as their body begins to feel the force of the winds from different directions. Those who become water elementals seem to have it the worse. Cyn Dal told me that they struggle to breathe to the point where they feel like they're drowning. They also suffer severe headaches because of the power of the tides. Once the suffering is over though, the elemental's powers come in full force."

"How old were you?" she asked quietly.

"Thirteen."

"I never felt any of those things," Elli whispered, feeling slightly ashamed that she had not gone through the same discomfort as her friends.

Turning his head and giving her a small smile that showed he understood the tone in her voice, he said, "Little wonder. You have more of Merlin's blood in your veins.

There was less normal blood to change into something magical."

"Was it painful?"

"Very. Everyone thought we had contracted some kind of disease and that we were going to die. We were in hospital together for those three days. If Blackwell hadn't been there, going through it with me...." Justin paused, his eyes going cloudy again as he turned back to look out the window. It had begun to rain, and little rivers of water were just beginning to form on the glass as it ran down. "I can remember when we first discovered our powers. Blackwell's parents were visiting us in hospital after our fever broke. They had stepped out of the room to talk to the doctor. His dad could be a little absent minded at times. He left his cigarette lighter on the bedside table, next to the chair he'd been sitting in. Bored, Blackwell picked it up and lit it. The fire flared and jumped from the lighter to his hand. We were both too shocked to scream. He closed his fist around it, and it went out. We looked at his hand but couldn't find any burns. I later found out that I could do the same thing.

"Once we found out that we could both control fire, we thought we were, as Americans say, 'real bad asses.' I'll spare you the details save it to say we did what we wanted, when we wanted for the most part. Blackwell and I became even more inseparable... or at least we were until bloody Nigel Clandestine came into the picture." Pausing, Justin turned around and leaned against the wall, keeping his arms crossed as he continued his story. "We'd heard about this new place in the lower rent district called 'The Club' run by a Nigel Clandestine. The word on the street was it was a really tough place. The bloke who told us about it really talked it up, saying how much we'd like it and how great Clandestine and his club were. Blackwell and I were fifteen and thought we could handle it, so we went.

"At the time, we thought we were the only two in the world who had abilities. We were dead wrong. 'The Club' was a place for elementals only, and the bloke who'd talked it up so much turned out to be one of the leaders, Pelt. He'd recognized our abilities and wanted us to join. That was when I first met Arnie Klimet and Daniel Quillet. Quillet wasn't called Ash yet. He was given that nickname by Clandestine later. They were just kids with bad backgrounds looking for something to cling to.

"'The Club' was also where I met Clandestine and his other allies – Bellstone, Kraller, Yarrow, and Drailinger – though they weren't as polished as they are now. Basically, they were a bunch of fanatics. When I first met Clandestine, he kept going on and on about how the world was falling apart, and it was up to him and the others to make order out of chaos. Don't get me wrong. It was seductive, but I didn't buy into it. I mean, any guy who offers world domination up to a teenage kid is either crazy or peddling more than encyclopedias.

"Blackwell though? He fell for that trash right off. He became obsessed and Clandestine fed into that. He began urging Blackwell into trying to groom his powers and make them stronger."

Justin paused for a moment, as if searching for the right words. His disdain for Derek was obvious as he continued, albeit haltingly, "And then one night he got to put all that hard work to the test. He and Ash and a couple of the other members set fire to a building when one of the tenants, a moderate elemental with only a trickle of air power, refused to join 'The Club.' It was a message to anyone who turned down an 'invitation' to Clandestine's party. Most of the people got out. All except this... little kid."

Justin's voice became heavy with emotion as Elli felt him relive that night, his eyes distant. She felt her own heart contract in sympathy and bit her lip to keep her own feelings that were bubbling inside from emerging.

Swallowing the lump in his throat, Justin continued, "I tried to save him, but I just wasn't strong enough then. I was barely able to control the fire enough to get in the building and find him. I carried him outside. My God, Elli, he was... his skin...." When Justin couldn't finish the sentence, Elli went to him and put her arms around his neck. He clung to her like she was his only shield against the memories. "He died in my arms," Justin whispered. "He looked up into my eyes and just went out. And when he died, a part of me died. That poor, little kid had never done anything to anyone, and Blackwell and Clandestine had killed him for no reason other than this damn war."

Pulling back just enough to look into her green eyes, he proceeded, his voice cold. "When I confronted Blackwell, it was like he had no conscience at all. He said that kid was just a casualty in the battle against chaos. He might as well have been talking about the bloody weather for all the emotion he showed. He asked me where my loyalties laid. Every cell in my body wanted to fry him on the spot, but I knew that if I acted, I'd lose any chance of getting Clandestine, too. So, I walked away and waited. During that time, I watched their movements from the shadows. I did what I could to keep them from gaining more followers, but there weren't many who would listen to me. Saving even one was a small triumph but put me at a great risk. I left home so my parents wouldn't be caught up in everything. I worked on my powers in secret until... until Mum and Dad were killed by a drunk driver."

Knowing the same loss, Elli kept silent but wrapped her arms around him tighter and laid her head against his chest. She felt the same hollowness inside at hearing about his parents as she'd felt when hers had died.

"I was almost seventeen when I lost my parents. I thought I had no family left until my grandmother sent for me. I knew nothing about her since she and my parents had been estranged. When I came to Ravenwood, she helped me develop my powers. She told me about you and my destiny.

"It was just before my eighteenth birthday when I heard word that Clandestine had grown so powerful that he had set up a new base of operations in the country. He must have done his research since the old convent he chose must have been originally built by Celtic elementals. There are signs of it all over the school if you know what to look for. It wouldn't have been the first place that started off in the hands of pagans and was transformed by the Church.

"Whatever its origins, it was the perfect place for Clandestine's plans. He bought it and turned it into a school where he could gather more elementals in the open instead of resorting to rundown buildings in back alleys. It was the beginning of my senior year. I scraped up all the money I could and paid the tuition. I've always believed in the philosophy of keeping your friends close, but your enemies closer."

"It must have been hard seeing Derek for the first time after all of that," Elli said, her voice quiet as she looked up at him.

"Actually, what's hard is describing how I felt. He'd become Clandestine's second in command, and he didn't trust me anymore than I trusted him. But the esteemed Dean Clandestine, as he now called himself, convinced Blackwell that I could be swayed to their way of thinking. We watched each other like hawks. Over the course of the year, more students came to the school, and the dean started sifting through them like a gold miner. He added Mark and Cami to his arsenal. But while Clandestine gathered his army, I searched for mine. That's how I met others who wanted to see Clandestine stopped."

"Page, Branda, Cyn Dal and Teddy," Elli said, receiving a nod of confirmation.

"Clandestine had Yarrow follow the lineages of those known to have received Merlin's powers and then sent letters to their descendants about how prestigious the school was. Cyn Dal and Page's parents jumped at the chance of sending them. For those who couldn't afford the tuition, Clandestine sweetened the deal by offering scholarships. That's how Teddy and Branda came to the school. Teddy's family owns a flower shop in Georgia, and Branda was living in foster care in South Africa."

"But if the school is a gathering place for Merlin's descendants, why are there so few who are aware of it? Why are the numbers on both sides so small?" Elli asked, trying to put the final pieces of the puzzle together.

"My grandmother says it isn't an automatic thing for the descendants to come into their powers. Over time, the lineages die out or the power becomes something like a recessive gene. Parents or lines that have strong elemental children may only have a touch of power here or there, but it is mostly shrugged off or excused. You've heard of gardeners having 'green thumbs' or dancers being 'lighter than air', right?"

Receiving a nod from Elli in confirmation, Justin continued, "Those people tend to have gifts but don't realize it. That's why there were so many students at Clandestine University who are blind to what they truly are. Since there are no guarantees that the descendants inherit any powers, it was a gamble on Clandestine's part each time he contacted one of them. Sometimes he won, and sometimes he lost.

"To keep up appearances, the school couldn't send all of them home, so some were allowed to stay but were kept in the dark about their ancestry or the goings on there. If one did surface but had too few powers to be useful in the coming war, they were stripped of their powers in a very painful process and were sent home."

"Then why didn't the Acolytes do that to you or Page and the others?"

"Because Clandestine saw our strength, and the purity of our powers, and didn't want to see them annihilated. Instead he allowed us to stay, arrogantly thinking that we would join him in the end. And so, we stayed and waited for you. We watched as Blackwell and the others destroyed lives, and we were helpless to stop it because we weren't whole without you," Justin explained.

"But why didn't the authorities come and stop him? There's no way the dean could have silenced that many witnesses. Even if he scared the students into silence, what about the people he left behind in London?"

"They were made to forget," Justin said, deadpanned.

"Forget how?" Elli asked, a coldness creeping up her

spine.

"Water elementals can control more than rivers and rain," he replied. "The human brain is surrounded by water. Those without abilities to protect them...." Justin trailed off, not needing to finish the statement. Elli shuddered, remembering the white, bonefish-like looks of her old classmates as the Acolytes controlled their minds.

Putting his hand on her cheek, Justin looked intently into her green eyes. "Now you see, love. You can't save Blackwell because he doesn't really want to be saved. He helped Clandestine and the Acolytes grow fat and happy off the suffering of the others. His soul was perverted the minute he let that kid die. He took away my life, and now he's trying to take you away from me, too."

There, he'd said it. And once those words were out, Elli felt as though all the air in the room had grown heavy and stagnant. Even as she stood within the circle of his arms, she knew that was what Justin was really afraid of. He thought Derek was going to take her away from him. He'd finally let himself love after all those years of grief and loneliness, building an army to fight something he didn't even understand beyond the need to stop it. He'd lost his family to it. His life since childhood had been saturated with trying to stop the evil the dean had spawned. It was too much to ask of the nineteen-year-old Justin, let alone the fifteen-year-old one who had held a dying child in his arms while his friend looked on without pity.

Raising herself up on tiptoes, wanting to stop the anguish that almost glowed around him in waves of blue and gray, Elli kissed Justin ever so gently, her lips grazing his until he returned the gesture. He pressed her to him as she opened her mind, letting him feel her love as she spoke reassuringly to him. "*I am so sorry for what you've had to go through... so sorry. But Derek can't take me away from you. It's impossible. My heart is and always will be yours.*" She wandered through his thoughts, trying to wash away all the bad memories that streaked through his mind like black lightning.

She kissed them away, making roses and firelight bloom in the darkness. Pulling back, she looked into his eyes to find the hardness gone. It was replaced with a kind of wonder that she had only seen one time before. When their hearts had joined. *"Please understand that no matter what happens, I'm yours. I promise to take care of you."* Elli couldn't help the tinge of sadness that tickled at the edge of her mental voice. She knew she'd successfully kept her secret hidden from Justin while she'd walked through his memory, but the bitter sweetness of her promise brought it all back to her.

"What's wrong?" he asked, stroking her cheek.

"I have to ask you something that I know you aren't going to like. All I ask is that you trust me." Elli didn't trust her telepathic voice with what she was about to say. It opened her up to too many chances that Justin would see her terrible secret.

"With my life," he stated simply, not taking his eyes from hers.

Taking a deep breath, she said, "Let me try to help Derek. Please. I wish I could explain why I need to, but I can't. I don't even fully understand it myself. All I know is that I have to try. If he is as bad as his past proves him to be, then at least I won't have failed because I was too afraid to try. But I can't walk away. I can't let another person be burned by the dean like that boy you tried to save, not when I have a chance to stop it from happening. The Derek who helped you ward off those bullies is still in there, trying to make up for what he did. I've seen it. He saved me and now I have to try and save him." Elli waited for Justin to recoil from her. To yell and storm from the room. Instead, he only stared at her, his eyes still full of the same wonder mingled with a kind of resolution.

"You're determined, aren't you?" he asked after several heartbeats. When she nodded her answer, he sighed heavily, looked at the ceiling as if he was searching for patience from above, and then finally returned his eyes to her. "All right, love. I don't like this. In fact, I hate this. But I trust you and am willing to go along with you on this one." Seeing her about to speak, Justin shook his head. "On two conditions. The first is that we don't share any kind of information regarding our plans with Blackwell. I want him kept in the dark as much as possible, and I don't want him anywhere near Merlin's crystal. The second is that if I have any inkling that he's trying to betray us, you leave him to me. I won't risk your life even if you're willing to. Is it a deal?"

After giving him a brief kiss, Elli smiled, linking her hands around his back. "Deal."

A sound like nails on a chalk board came from the window, startling them. They both stared in awe as the rivers of rain began to run together, making a solid sheet of water that covered the outside of the window. It almost looked like someone had taken an old-style mirror, the kind with wavy imperfections in it, and placed it against the window, facing in.

In the water, they saw the faces of some of the Acolytes reflected back at them, as if they were ghosts, their images blurring and shifting as the water ran down the window. They saw Mr. Pelt, his pudgy chin stubbled with several days' beard; Mr. Drailinger's skull-colored face; and Ms. Bellstone wearing a garish, octopus-inspired necklace around her throat.

Intermingled with them were images of some of the students who had joined their side. But in front of them all, holding the same knife he'd used to scratch the window pane with, was the dean, his face cracked in a wicked smile as he played the tip of the knife between two fingers. Though none of the images spoke, the sight of them made the message ring loud and clear. They were watching Elli and her friends. They were still hunting them. They always would be.

With a growl, Justin grabbed a book from the bedside table and flung it. It broke through the glass and into the watery window, making the images disappear as the water dispersed.

Shaking a little at the thought of them watching from afar, Elli and Justin said nothing as they clung to each other. Water droplets gave off a soft "plink, plink" sound as they were cut in half on the sharp window's edge, spraying Justin and Elli as they held on to each other.

Chapter 12

The ocean's spray filled Elli's senses as she stood on the
bow of the *Lois Jane*. A joyful Toby stood at her side, wagging
his tail as his tags jingled in the wind. Even though they had
only been at sea for two days, Elli couldn't get past the urge
that she was racing to meet her destiny on the dark water. It
was like Merlin's crystal was calling to her, beckoning. She'd
felt it the morning she'd woken in Justin's arms in the little
village inn, and it was with her even now. The others seemed
to feel it that first morning, too, as it had been easier than she'd
thought to wake everyone and get them down to the docks on
time. It was like they also felt the pull.

As they had all boarded, Cyn Dal took her post as
navigator next to Tom in the steerage compartment, keeping to
the plan that the book would be kept hidden but referred to
often, so they didn't drift off course. Once the lines had been
cast, the *Lois Jane* had roared to life, her engines smoky but
running, and the group had begun their quest by sea.

Even Justin and Derek had been subdued in the need to
get going. They had barely said a word to each other, which
Elli took to be a good sign. After all, anything was better than
listening to them bicker. Though Cyn Dal, Branda, Page and

Teddy had voiced their opinions and worries about Derek to
her through their telepathic link, they had finally consented to
his going with them when Justin explained his conditions. It
was plainly obvious that even though the four disliked Derek
and didn't trust him any farther than they could throw him, they
didn't have the pure hatred for him that Justin did.

Elli knew they believed she was being naive about the
situation, but they were willing to give him the benefit of the
doubt for her sake, and she appreciated that more than she
could say. One thing was for sure, though. She was going to
confront their newest member about his past the first chance
she got.

A bark from Toby brought Elli back to the present. The
roll of the sea was comforting. The sky was as overcast as it
had been two days ago, the clouds steel gray. After giving the
dog a quick scratch behind the ears, she made her way to the
helm, Toby at her heels. Tom had stowed his fishing nets
away, making movement on the deck much easier. Once
inside, she found Cyn Dal pouring over a map, her dark hair
swaying with the rock of the ship. Tom stood at the wheel,
staring out at the open ocean. The sound of her friends' voices
drifted up from the open door that led down into the galley.
Toby curled up in his little corner bed, watching the three with
his big, brown eyes.

"How are we doing?" Elli asked Cyn Dal, peering at the
nautical map on the table, the latest book direction outlined in
red. Though the book had sent them straight west for the first
day, it had suddenly veered northwest at around noon on the
second.

"All right, but Tom's a little worried about the weather.
He thinks we might be heading for a storm."

Walking over to stand next to him, Elli peered at the
man's face. "A bad one?" she asked.

"Well, lass, it's hard to say. The sky looks threatening,
but I've seen the blackest of clouds give off only a refreshing
rain. The water is quite choppy and the wind's picked up
which aren't good signs, but none of the instruments or the

coast guard are predicting anything. It's strange to say the least." Tom's voice sounded uncertain, but he gave her a reassuring smile. "I wouldn't worry about it though, lass. This old boat of mine has weathered squalls before and lived to tell the tale. It's likely that we won't hit anything but a little wind and rain."

Nodding her head, Elli returned his smile with a half-hearted one of her own. Taking hold of the rope banister that lead below deck, she emerged into the galley to find Branda and Derek making sandwiches for lunch. Justin sat at the little table, a book of sailing knots open before him and a small length of rope in his hands. A soft groan from the back bunks called to Elli. Stepping past Branda and Derek, she made her way toward the sound.

"How's he doing?" she asked, taking a seat beside Page on a bunk opposite Teddy.

Placing a cold rag on his forehead, Page shook her head. "He seems to be doing a little better," she said. "At least he's stopped –" When Teddy groaned, Page didn't finish her sentence. Teddy's sea sickness had developed as soon as the *Lois Jane* had left the harbor. Cyn Dal, Page, and Elli had been taking turns at his side, but there was little to do but wait it out.

"Poor Teddy," Elli said. "Nothing like being sea sick."

"Haven't you ever been on a boat before?" Page teased lightly, giving him a cool drink.

"Hey, I'm earth, remember? Water and I make mud." His voice was rough, but apparently his sense of humor was left untouched by his current discomfort.

"Oh, I can't wait to tell Cyn Dal what you said!" Page squeaked, winking at Elli when Teddy winced.

"Anyone hungry?" Derek asked, poking his head into the bunk area, a plate of sandwiches in his hand. He gave the plate to Page who offered one to Teddy. Instead of taking it, Teddy covered his nose and mouth with his hand.

"Oops! Sorry," Derek said sheepishly, taking the food back. Looking at Elli, he said, "Can't you heal him?"

"I wanted to try when we first set out, but he wouldn't let

me. He said it wasn't that serious. Just uncomfortable."

"I imagine you're kicking yourself for that right about now, aren't you?" Derek said, smiling at Teddy who only groaned a reply. "Maybe you should heal him anyway, even if he doesn't want you to. Who knows what we might come up against, and it isn't good for one of us to be out of commission."

"I think he's right," Page said, eyeing Teddy who merely groaned with discomfort. "Besides, then he'll have to help out like the rest of us."

Derek replied with a laugh, "Then maybe that's the real reason he didn't want to be healed. He liked the idea of you girls taking care of him."

Teddy cleared his throat uncomfortably and said in a raspy voice, "You'll need a cup of hot water and some mint. There should be a few leaves in the first aid kit in my bag."

"Are you sure I can do this?" Elli hesitated, "I mean I've never... I mean I don't know how to heal someone."

"Relax. I'll tell you how, step by step. Maybe –" Teddy's sentence was cut off by a sudden dip of the ship that made cold sweat pop out on his forehead and gave him a definite green hue. "Maybe it's a good thing that I'm your first patient since I know what to expect."

Nervous but determined, Elli pulled Teddy's bag from the compartment under his bunk while Page went to get the water. Digging around in it, her hand brushed up against the rough texture of a wooden box which she pulled out. A first aid cross had been burned into the cover. The smell of dried herbs wafted over Elli as she opened it, reminding her of the scent that always seemed to linger on Teddy's clothes. Small packets of plants, everything from chamomile to rosemary, were organized into neat little rows next to a few gauze bandages and some surgical tape. Smiling as she pulled a few springs of mint from the box, Elli realized that she should have known that Teddy's first aid kit would have been more than Band-Aids and an ice pack. She carefully closed and repacked the box.

"What do I do first?"

"Pull the leaves from the stems and place the mint leaves whole in the water. Stir it carefully. The point is to get them to naturally leach out their essence, not to pound it out of them." While following Teddy's directions, Elli created a weak mint tea which she gave him to drink. Then, taking the wet leaves from the bottom of the cup, she rubbed them on the palms her hands, letting the essence of the plant seep into her skin. Closing her eyes, she placed one hand on his forehead and one on his stomach. The scent of mint filled the small bunk area as she searched for the emerald in her mind.

It was a strange feeling to heal someone. Through her closed eyelids, she saw Teddy's body as layers of tissue, bone, and muscle with veins, like little highways, carrying blood from his heart to his limbs and brain and back again. In his mind she saw Cyn Dal, kind and gentle as she smiled at him. Teddy saw her as beautiful and warm, like coming home. Her eyes sparkling as she looked up at him. His chocolate-colored hand covering her small, ivory one. Realizing that she had accidentally entered Teddy's private thoughts, Elli backed out quickly, feeling her own cheeks grown warm, and set about trying to cure Teddy's sea sickness.

Concentrating, she felt a slight tingling in her hands as the healing power of the mint was amplified and sent into Teddy. She willed her power to make him well. Elli felt her earth magic spread through her friend's body. She imagined that she had the power to mend broken bones and heal torn muscle. She saw herself chasing away viruses and making Teddy strong again. In her mind, the sea sickness was a monster that she could blow away with the slightest breath. It was nothing compared to her ability to heal. She could cure headaches and heartburn. She was Florence Nightingale with the power to erase disease from the face of the world.

"Um, Elli?" Page said, her voice barely registering to Elli who was still deep in her magic. "You might want to quit now. Teddy only had a stomach ache. He didn't need his kidneys repaired or anything."

Opening her eyes, Elli saw Teddy floating before her, his

whole body encased in a bright, green light.

"Mind letting me down?" he asked, his voice healthy and hearty. Embarrassed again, Elli quickly drew her powers back into herself, realizing her mistake only after Teddy landed on the bed from his high perch.

"Sorry," she said, blushing as he sat up. "How do you feel?"

"Like I could run up Everest without stopping for breath. That was some pretty potent healing. I've never seen or experienced anything quite like it."

"It was strange to watch, too. You two were glowing. I mean as in light bulbs! I know that Teddy and Marion usually glow when they heal, but nothing like that. I almost needed my sunglasses because it was so bright."

"Now that the patient is healed," Derek began, handing the plate of sandwiches to Teddy who proceeded to scarf them down one by one, "Elli, can I talk to you for a second on deck?"

"Sure." Passing behind Branda as she followed Derek toward the stairs, Elli caught Justin's eye.

"Where are you going?" he asked, letting the knot he was trying to tie slip from his fingers.

"Up on deck. Got a problem with that?" Derek jeered.

"With you going up on deck, no. With you being alone with my girl, yes."

Glancing at his watch, Derek replied, "Hey look, you're a few decades late for the Women's Rights Movement. She isn't property anymore."

"You know, while you're up there, why don't you just jump overboard and save us all a lot of grief."

"But you'd miss me too much."

"Bloody hell, will you two knock it off!" Branda exclaimed, tossing the rag she'd been using to wipe up crumbs with into the sink. "I swear this rust bucket just isn't big enough for the two of you."

"Good point. Maybe we should take it outside. Come on, Lady Allison," Derek replied as he climbed the steps.

Cutting Justin's retort off, Elli said, "You promised. If I can't even talk to him, how can I help him?"

"You're not going anywhere alone with him," Justin said with gritted teeth as he slid out from behind the table. "I'm going with you."

"Fine," she answered. Derek was waiting for her at the top of the stairs. She followed him toward the bow of the *Lois Jane*, Justin on her heels. Giving him a look, Justin leaned up against the front of the steerage compartment, crossing his arms with agitation. His position was close enough to satisfy his need to keep her safe, but far enough away so that Elli and Derek would have some privacy if they spoke low.

"He's more protective than a mother hen," Derek said, gesturing toward Justin's rigid form.

"Did you expect anything else?"

"No, actually. And I can't blame him, really. If," Derek began, his voice going soft, his dark hair blending with the darkening sky, "If I had someone to care about like that and I knew they were in any danger, I'd never let them out of my sight either."

The sound of Justin clearing his throat caught Elli's attention. She leaned against the railing and tried to change the subject, "So, what did you want to talk to me about?"

Shoving his hands in his pockets, Derek said, "I just wanted to know how you talked the others into letting me come along?"

"You mean you want to know how I got Justin to agree." When he didn't answer, Elli took his silence as a 'yes.' "Well, we had a long discussion about – about how I wanted to help you. How I wanted to repay you for saving my life." Elli hoped that Derek didn't hear the hesitation in her voice. With Justin looking on, she wasn't exactly ready to bring up Derek's past. She thought it would be more comfortable to wait until they didn't have such a prying audience, but since this little adventure started, her comfort was a luxury that she didn't seem to be able to afford.

"Give me a little more credit, Lady Allison. What did

you two *really* talk about?"

Not sure how to bring up the topic, Elli remained quiet. She had promised herself that she would ask him at her earliest opportunity, but she had hoped it would be on her own terms. Sighing heavily, she thought to herself, *Oh, well, I might as well jump in with both feet. That way if the earth opens up, I won't touch the muddy side walls.* Aloud she said, "Justin and I talked about how you two grew up together. He told me how you joined the dean and all the bad things you did. He explained how the university came about and how it all started as a club in the middle of the London low rent district. And... other things."

"You mean how I ruined his life. How I killed that little kid." Derek's voice was as emotionless as his dark eyes were piercing. Taking his hands out of his pockets, Derek crossed his arms. *Funny how he and Justin both do that when they're angry,* she thought.

"He said that you set the fire," she said, her voice almost inaudible in the rising din of waves and wind.

"And you believed him. I thought you knew me better."

"I don't know what to believe. I wasn't there. All I know is that Justin thinks you betrayed him, and it has had a dramatic effect on his life. He's had so much pain."

"You think my life has been easy!" he threw back, his voice low but harsh. Closing his eyes, he waited for several moments. "I'm sorry, Elli," he began more gently as he looked at her again, "that wasn't fair. You're right. Justin has had a hard life, and I know he blames me for it. But before you pass judgment on me, can I tell you a secret? After all, since I know one of yours, you should know one of mine."

Nodding her consent, he continued, "I want to tell you the truth about what happened the night of the fire. Ash, Walt Enterall, Patrick O'Neill, and I were sent by Clandestine to this little apartment building to talk to an air elemental about joining 'The Club.' Talk. That's all we were supposed to do. Well, when he refused, Ash got this bright idea that we should make an example of him. Before I could stop him, he pulled up a fireball and tossed it at the curtains. They caught right away. I didn't even have time to react before Ash and the other guys were hauling me out of the building. I didn't know that Justin had gone in until I saw him running out the door with the kid under his arm."

"Justin said that you acted like that little boy didn't mean anything. Like he was just a casualty of war."

"I had to say that. I could feel Ash and the others behind me, and I had to act that way. If Clandestine questioned my loyalty, he'd never stop hunting me until I was dead. That's what happened to Walt and Patrick. After the fire, their guilt got the better of them and they wanted out. Clandestine gave them their wish and he let them *out*." The hard glint in Derek's eyes and his emphasis on the word 'out' told Elli that he didn't mean alive.

"But you've betrayed the dean? Won't he go after your family?"

"My father is too politically powerful, and Clandestine knows it. In fact, that's partially why he made me his second. He was counting on my father's political connections to help him rule. Clandestine would never threaten that."

After a moment of silence, Elli said quietly, her eyes distant, "So it was Ash who killed that little boy." It was possible that Justin had been mistaken about the fire. Thinking back to the cold, immovable character that was Daniel "Ash" Quillet, the possibility seemed to strengthen. But then a thought came to her, making her eyes lock with his again, "What about after you became second in command? What about the elementals who had their powers stripped so the Acolytes could become stronger? What about those lives that were destroyed?"

Pausing for a minute, he ran his hands through his hair. The movement was agitated, as if he wanted to reach out for her to try and make her understand but knew he couldn't. Instead, in his anxiety, his words came out in a rush of emotion. "I *have* done some bloody terrible things in order to survive. I did help Clandestine and the others strip the powers.

I know it was wrong, and there isn't a day that goes by that I don't regret everything I've done. Sometimes at night I still hear the screaming. It haunts me and that's why I'm trying to atone. That's why I left Clandestine. That's why I risked almost certain death at the hands of the Acolytes to help you. I had to help you because I... because I have to make up for my hand in all this! It's small consolation that I talked the dean into letting those poor bastards live after he sucked them dry. I am so sorry that little kid died, and that Justin has had a rotten life. I'd take it all back in a heartbeat if I could."

The anguish in Derek's voice cut at Elli's heart. She felt the burn of tears in her eyes. She longed to cry. To cry for Justin and the life he lost. For that little child who was caught in the crossfire. For Derek who wanted so bad to fix his mistakes. And in an instant, she was angry, so angry that she wanted to scream as the tears dried up in the heat of her fury.

"How dare the dean treat people this way, like they're puppets! They aren't tissues he can just wad up and throw away when he's done. It isn't right! He has to be stopped and I am going to stop him if it's the last thing I do." She pounded her fist on the railing of the boat to emphasize her point.

"Just make sure it *isn't* the *last* thing," Derek said quietly, placing a hand on her arm, her anger congealing in her surprise.

"What do you bloody well think you're doing?" Justin spat as he crossed the deck. Elli felt the bow of the ship rock sharply, but the rage in Justin's eyes seemed a closer danger than the rolling sea.

Pulling his hand back as if he'd been bitten, Derek glared at Justin. "Need something, warden?"

"Don't push me, Blackwell, or you'll find your arse on fire," Justin growled.

"You're welcome to try," Derek replied, his eyes narrowing and a sneer crossing his face.

"Touch her again and I'll do more than try." The danger in Justin's voice was palpable even over the roar of the water

"Stop it!" Elli shouted, throwing her hands up in the air

with exasperation. Both turned to look at her, shocked expressions on their faces. "The enemy is out there. Not here. If you
two don't cool off, I'm going to throw you both overboard and
don't think I can't!"

As her words sunk in, a large wave crashed over the bow,
drenching them. "You might not have to throw us over. It
looks like Mother Nature is going to do it for you!" Derek said
as another wave hit them hard. Whipping her wet hair out of
her face, Elli stared up into the turbulent skies as they shifted
and dipped in a violent ballet. The sound of thunder and the
flash of lightning filled the air as the bow plummeted beneath
their feet. Grabbing the railing, Elli hung on as the deck rushed
up to meet her again.

"Everyone on deck!" Branda yelled through their link.
The sound of the wind and the waves filled Elli's senses as rain
began to pour in sheets down on them.

Turning her head, she saw Tom frantically trying to steer
the *Lois Jane* into the waves to keep her from capsizing. Cyn
Dal and Teddy stood beside him, their features obscure in the
wash running down the pane. On the main deck, Branda stood
holding on to the metal frame of the steerage compartment, her
face set in a barbaric grin. She screamed her delight as the boat
dipped and swayed in the storm, rain and wind lashing their
bodies with saltwater as another wave crashed down on the
deck. Page sat, huddled with her arms wrapped around the side
railing of the ship at about mid-deck. A loud roar and the
pummeling of a wave made Elli's arms ache as she gripped the
railing, her vision blurring as her world was filled with the
white of the water which pounded her to her knees.

The sound of wood cracking made Elli's head snap back
up just in time to see the railing Page had been holding on to
break away and a wave bare down on the girl's small form,
slamming her head into the side wall of the boat. Page now lay
on the deck; her unconscious form was being whipped around
like a rag doll's as another wave rushed over the side.

"Page!" Elli screamed as she crawled to her feet.
Hanging on to what was left of the railing, she tried to make

her way to Page's small form, afraid that the next wave would wash her friend away. As the boat pitched, Elli felt herself begin to topple forward off the slippery deck. A strong arm wrapped itself around her waist and pulled her back.

"What are you doing?" Justin hollered, holding her.

"Let me go! Page needs help." The frantic look of torn emotions crossed Justin's face at the double jeopardy of it all. Staying meant the possibility of losing Page but going meant the possibility of losing Elli.

"Help Page!" Derek yelled as he moved toward them, his eyes flashing with the lightning. "I'll take care of Elli." With a look at Derek that said, "You'd better," Justin reluctantly let go and began to make his way toward Page, his feet slipping and sliding out from under him on the writhing deck. In the end, he had to crawl the last few feet to her when the boat made a particularly hard plunge.

"*Teddy, Page is hurt!*" Justin exclaimed telepathically as he reached Page.

Elli barely had enough time to see Teddy turn and stagger his way out of the steerage compartment before she heard Derek yell, "Look out!" Grabbing Elli and bracing her against the side with his body, Derek's arms locked protectively around her as a monstrous wave toppled down on the *Lois Jane*. Elli, feeling her feet start to slip from under her, clung to the railing.

"That was close!" Derek yelled in her ear.

Saltwater stung her eyes as she peered forward into the gloom. In the small space of a breath, pure terror rippled through her body like the venom from a striking snake. A waterspout, which reached from the top of the towering waves to the ink-black sky, formed before her eyes, swirling and spitting as it neared the ship. A scream lodged in Elli's throat as her insides turned to quicksand. She barely heard Derek swear as the din around them amplified.

"*Cyn Dal, can you stop it?*" Justin yelled as he and Teddy tried to carry Page toward the aft in hopes of getting her inside the steerage compartment, the onslaught of waves fighting them. The groups' telepathic web rang with urgency.

"*I can't!*" the girl replied, her voice nearly choking with panic. "*It isn't acting like a true spout. It's as if it's laced with a magic too powerful for me to tamper with.*"

Staring up at the storm and the deadly, watery tube before her, Elli knew that it was too powerful for her as well.

"*It's the Acolytes again!*" Branda yelled. "*They're trying to drown us!*"

"*It's not the Acolytes! This thing feels older. Whatever magic is keeping it together is as old as time!*" Cyn Dal hollered.

As the spout grew nearer and she could make out the writhing shapes beneath its surface, Elli knew with unflinching certainty that they were all going to die. Everything became crystal clear to her. She hardly noticed the waves constantly drenching her or the sting of the salt on her skin. She didn't feel Derek's arms around her as he kept her from being sucked away. The waterspout was all that mattered. It encased her entire vision. As the spout picked the *Lois Jane* up, Elli felt her friends scream in terror through their link as the sounds of water, cracking wood and twisting metal filled all her senses.

She gripped the paint-splintered railing as the insane calm that enveloped her made her stinging eyes notice the oddity of her surroundings. It was strange how, even though there was so little light, the surface of the water shimmered like oil on water. Elli imagined that she could even see fish swimming around inside the spout. A pair of brilliant, aquamarine eyes seemed to flash in the blue lightning where the top of the spout met the darkness above.

It was then that Elli knew what to do. With the clarity of a premonition, one which burst through her thoughts like an explosion, she understood what the storm was and how she could stop it The Lady had told her to choose, to choose between running from what she was or accepting it and all its consequences... perhaps even her own death. It was time to make that choice.

"Derek, I have to stand up!" she yelled in his ear.

"Are you bloody crazy?"

"I have to or we're all going to die!" Though it only took a moment for Derek to decide, it was long enough for Elli's insides to churn with urgency. Receiving a nod, her heart beating so fast it made her dizzy with adrenaline, Elli pulled herself up. She felt herself being lifted up off the deck and Justin's cry in her mind as he felt helpless to go to her. Grabbing her around the waist before she could fly away from him, Elli saw the taught sinews in Derek's arm as he fought to hold her to him with one arm and anchor them to the boat with the other.

Knowing she only had a moment, Elli opened her mind at the same time she screamed at the top of her lungs, "Godmother, I've chosen!"

A sound like 'so be it' rang around her, and the sudden sensation of falling made Elli's breath catch in her throat and her stomach clench as the *Lois Jane* plummeted from the skies. She gripped the railing again and felt Derek pull her closer to him, trying to protect her from whatever would happen next. Squeezing her eyes shut, Elli whispered an 'I love you' to Justin as the sound of waves and the enormous reverberation of crashing water made her ears roar.

Chapter 13

Elli waited for the pain to come, but it never did. With her green eyes still squeezed tightly shut, she began to notice other sensations through the cloud of dizziness that always seemed to follow a huge jolt of adrenaline. She could still feel the roughness of the *Lois Jane*'s railing under her fingers and Derek's chest rising and falling with every breath. But, why didn't she feel any pain? Why wasn't she treading water right now? Praying that she wasn't dead, she opened her eyes to the sight of the sun reflecting off a calm sea and a bright sky. The cackling of a gull tickled her ears.

"Are we dead?" Derek asked, releasing her so he could sag to the deck with exhaustion.

"I don't think so." Feeling the wetness of her shirt and the squish of her feet in her shoes, Elli smiled. "I don't think heaven is this moist. We must have made it through."

"I take back every bad thing I said about this boat," Branda said, wringing the water from her emerald-green shirt and smiling. "In fact, I'm naming all my kids Lois Jane."

"That might be kind of hard for the boys to live down," Elli replied with a laugh.

"So, I'll pay for counseling."

The sound of a groan caught Elli's attention and she quickly made her way to the aft of the ship, Derek and Branda trailing behind. When they rounded the corner, they found Page, her hand on her head, lying against Justin, her wet, red hair in tight, spiral curls. Teddy sat next to her, his eyes closed. The tingle of earth energy tickled Elli's mind as she felt Teddy's power surrounding Page, making both healer and patient glow with a pale-green light that was dimmed by the sunshine.

"Are you okay?" Elli asked, kneeling next to her.

"Did someone get the license plate of the truck that ran me over?" Page's complexion was bleached-white, and her eyes seemed strangely dilated.

"I think she has a concussion," Teddy said, opening his eyes again.

"I'm fine," Page replied, trying to sit up. With a grunt, she fell back against Justin, her eyes glazing over. "Okay, maybe I'm not. Remind me not to do that again. It makes the world spin."

"Just be thankful that you only have a headache. If Elli hadn't seen you and warned me...," Justin said, his voice trailing off.

"Thanks," Page said, giving Elli a wobbly smile. Patting her friend reassuringly on the arm, Elli sat back on her heels just in time to see Justin pinning Derek with a look.

Clearing his throat, Justin said, his voice hesitant, "Thanks, Blackwell, for keeping Elli safe."

"What a sweet 'thank-you.' I'm touched," he replied, obviously aware of Justin's still undaunting reluctance to include him fully into their group.

"Just don't think I'm ready to pick out any bloody china patterns," Justin rebuked, his discomfort gone in a flash of arrogance.

Why do you have to fight even when you're thanking each other, Elli thought to herself, letting a sigh escape as she rolled her eyes. A soft groan from Page took her attention away from the two combatants. "Don't move. We'll get you fixed up," she said. Looking up at Teddy, she asked, "Where's Cyn Dal?"

Before he could answer, they heard Cyn Dal's frantic voice calling them telepathically. *"Everyone, hurry! You have to see this."* Leaving Page resting comfortably, Elli and the others hurried into the steerage compartment. They found Cyn Dal standing next to Tom, Merlin's history clutched to her chest. Toby sat beside Tom, a whining voice escaping his throat as he peered at his master. Aside from the strong smell of burnt oil in the air, nothing seemed out of the ordinary. Moving farther into the room, Elli noticed that Tom didn't turn to say anything to them. In fact, he seemed to be standing in a strange, stiff manner, his back completely straight, his hands still clenching the wheel, his red hair unmoving in the breeze that was circulating inside the small space. Peering into his face, Elli saw that his eyes were closed and there was a pleasant, almost peaceful, expression on his face... as if he'd just simply fallen asleep while steering.

"Is he dead?" Derek asked, waving his hand in front of Tom's face.

"No. I listened to his chest and I can still hear his heart beating," Cyn Dal explained.

"What happened?" Branda asked.

"It was so strange. When the spout spit us out, I found myself on the floor facing away from him. I was a little dazed. When I started talking to him to see if he was okay, he didn't answer. He just stood there. That's when I called. It's like he's been frozen in time." Toby whined again as if to confirm her story.

"Maybe it's a spell," Justin theorized.

"No, people always stand ramrod straight and sleep when they drive," Derek replied, his words marinated in sarcasm. He seemed unperturbed when Justin ignored him.

"I'll get my kit," Teddy said, disappearing down the steps to the galley. The others could hear the sounds of a little sloshing and rustling around, but the Georgia boy popped back up the stairs quickly. "It's a real mess down there. There's water everywhere."

"Was your kit spoiled?" Cyn Dal asked.

"Thankfully, no." Taking some sage from the wooden box, Teddy rubbed it on his hands and then placed them on Tom's arm and shoulder. The sensation of growing leaves and tilled earth once again tickled Elli's mind as she felt his power begin to work.

As they waited for his assessment, Cyn Dal gestured toward the control consul. "Look at that. The dials and everything are frozen, too. It's like both Tom and the *Lois Jane* are suspended while Toby and we are the only ones awake." Gazing at the board, Elli saw the truth in what she said. The engine light still shone bright green but there was no sound from below her feet. The oil pressure and gasoline gages remained steady. Picking up the CB mic, she pressed the button to speak but wasn't surprised when the bars on the radio remained constant.

"Not everything is frozen," Branda stated as she looked at the consul over Elli's shoulder. "The compass needle is spinning faster than a Vegas roulette wheel."

"Anyone else feel like we've just entered the Twilight Zone? Why is the clock on the dash still working perfectly when everything else isn't?" Justin asked.

"Maybe it's a sign that time is still going even if Tom and this boat aren't. Though I don't know how it happened, the date on my watch is different than when we went into the storm. It's like we've lost a day somewhere. It's been five days since we cracked the mystery of Merlin's book." Giving Elli a fleeting but meaningful look, Derek's message was clear, making her heart sink. The time limit was in effect even here... wherever 'here' was.

"You're as soaked as we all are," Justin said while gesturing at everyone's bedraggled appearance. "What makes you think your watch wouldn't be affected by the saltwater?"

"Because it's a *dive* watch, Spaller. In fact, it's the most expensive one money can buy." Before Justin could react to the connotation of the wealth reference, Derek continued,

"Even if the battery dies in it, it'll keep time through stored solar energy for up to thirty-six hours. Trust me. We've lost a day somewhere."

The sudden disappearance of the green aura surrounding Teddy and Tom caught their attention. Teddy wiped sweat beads from his forehead before letting his hands drop to his sides with exasperation. "Cyn Dal was right. He's alive and unharmed, but I don't understand what's happened to him. It's as if he's sleeping. I tried using the sage to wake him up, but he was totally unresponsive. Even people who are catatonic will send out a memory flash. I didn't even get a spark. Whatever caused this has the same feel of magic as the waterspout, old and powerful. There's nothing that we can do to help him."

"Except maybe to find Merlin's crystal," Derek said. The silence following his remark clung to them like their saturated clothing.

The soft texture of fur and the cold sensation of a nose on the palm of her hand made Elli look down to meet Toby's brown eyes. A small whine escaped his throat as she began to comfortingly scratch behind one of his ears. "Derek's right. Maybe the crystal can help him. We have to find it."

"And I know just where to look," Derek added, his dark eyes looking past them as he stared out the port window. Turning, Elli felt the telepathic link in her mind begin to vibrate with excitement as everyone began to talk at once.

"*Where did it come from?*"

"*I know it wasn't there a moment ago. I was just looking that way.*"

"*There's no way we could have missed it!*"

"*Oh, my God!*"

"*Look! Will you just look?*"

"*I can't believe it! We're here!*"

It was Page's foggy but anxious voice in their minds that stopped the stream of excited babble. "*What's taking you guys so long? What's happening?*" Page called, her telepathic voice foggy but anxious. "*Don't keep me in suspense or I'll have to crawl in there and find out for myself, concussion or no concussion.*"

Overwhelmed with relief, Elli found herself speaking aloud at the same time she answered Page telepathically, "It's an island."

Don't miss the third and final installment of The Clandestine Series – *The Betrayed.* Here is a sneak preview!

The Betrayed

Book Three in the Clandestine Series

by H.M. Kanicki

I dedicate this book to my soul mate – my loving husband – who believes in my dreams and helps me seek them out.

Chapter 1

"You don't think it's a mirage, do you?" Page asked, the sharp tang of willow bark still wafting around her, the scent the only reminder of her now-healed concussion. "You don't think that if we try and step on the land, it's going to disappear in a puff of smoke, and we'll be stuck in the middle of the ocean?"

Despite the need to assure Page that the island wasn't going to do any such thing, Elli remained silent. Not because she wanted to, but because she knew there were no more assurances anymore. She'd like to tell Page that an island couldn't do that. She'd like to tell her that it was impossible, but Elli knew she couldn't because it was all too possible, especially now. She'd learned all too well that what she used to think was logical, that what she used to know to be true, was all an illusion. Instead, it was the things that you thought to be impossible, that you believed at first to be simply tendrils of smoke, which were the only truly solid parts. It was strange to think that this earth-shattering realization had happened in a mere two weeks.

Has it really been such a short time?, Elli thought, surprised at how her life before Clandestine University seemed forever ago, like it was nothing but a dream and now that she was finally awake, inconsequential. Looking around at the others in the lifeboat with her, the full weight of what she was doing settled on her, making her hands tingle.

Looking over her shoulder at the *Lois Jane* as it slowly shrank in the distance, Elli sighed heavily. Absent mindedly petting Toby's soft fur coat, the dog sitting quietly beside her, his pink tongue lolling from his mouth, she felt a twinge of guilt leaving Tom, their newly petrified ship's captain, on the boat all alone. But, as Derek had rationally explained as he'd led her to the small craft which was being loaded with all the supplies she and her six companions could carry, there was little they could do for him. Whatever power that was holding him in suspended animation was one that they couldn't tamper with or reverse.

"The best way to help Tom is to find Merlin's crystal. It's our only hope," he'd said while helping her into the lifeboat. *Merlin's crystal.* Now there was a phrase she never thought she'd utter in her life – even in her mind! Okay, so Elli Wafe had been born with the special powers of precognition. So, she had spent her life running from the visions which invaded her mind and frightened her with their intensity and accuracy. But being the long-lost ancestor of a court magician and the Goddaughter of the Lady of the Lake, a watery creature that wasn't even supposed to exist, seemed a bit much.

To make matters worse, she and her friends had the ultimate destiny of saving the world from a band of lunatic sorcerers who theatrically called themselves the Acolytes. *Who would've thought that I, a nobody from nowhere, would wind up saving the world*, Elli thought, hearing the sarcasm in her own mental voice.

But, hidden deep under the sarcasm and the self-doubt, Elli felt a small twinge of hope, especially as she looked at her friends around her. They'd been through so much already, this band of haphazard teenagers. Teddy Koran, a mahogany-skinned Georgia boy who was big enough to play for the Packers, with the power of earth and the strength of growing things. Branda Aster, blue-eyed, fair skinned, a tattoo of an intertwined dragon and a phoenix running up her arm to come to a rest on her cheek, symbolic of her powers over flame. Page Fellor, a modern-day, red-headed Irish pixie with the element of air. Cyn Dal Roster, her almond shaped eyes glowing with the kindness of gentle rain. Justin Spaller, their leader and her only love, fiery and devoted. Derek Blackwell....

It was hard to sum Derek up into a nifty little verse of characteristics. He was secretive, like the blaze that hid beneath the mast on the forest floor. He was the fire that destroyed your house and the candle you lit from the flames of it, trying to make some good out of all the destruction caused.

And then, there was herself. Allison Wafe or Elli for short, with the powers of all the elements combined into one package, but with only the slightest notion of how to use them. She'd accepted her destiny, yet acceptance didn't lead to direct knowledge of the abilities running through her veins or a perfect cure for the little kernel of doubt in her mind that wanted so desperately to grow and consume her.

But, in spite of it all, here she was with her friends, on the way to fulfill that self-same destiny, hoping that God didn't make a mistake in choosing her. The weight of the world was a lot to bear, especially this early in the morning.

The sound of the bottom of the boat scrapping on the sand of the beach made goosebumps raise on Elli's arms and jarred her from her thoughts. Looking up, she saw Justin hesitate, his foot on the bow, Page's words obviously having an effect.

"Well, Spaller, aren't you going to jump?" Derek chided, a smug smile across his face.

"Be my guest," Justin shot back.

"And risk taking your Neil Armstrong moment of being the first person in a few hundred years to set foot on the Lady's island? No, thanks. Fame and fortune? They aren't my thing."

"Yeah, right," Justin replied, his sarcasm rank.

"I'll go first," Elli broke in, making her way to the bow, the sound of Toby's tags jingling as he followed her. "I've spent three days on a very small ship with you two bickering like a couple of old ladies, and I'm not about to spend another two in an even smaller boat." As she prepared herself to jump, she felt a strong hand on her forearm.

"Not so fast, love," Justin replied, ignoring Toby's growl at the way he was holding her. "If anyone's taking the chance on this thing going 'poof,' it's going to be me." Without another word, Justin lept into the surf, and to everyone's amazement ... he didn't sink. Instead, he stood on very wet, very real sand and breathed a sigh of relief.

"So, you going to pull us more securely on to shore or just stand there washing your feet?" Derek remarked, leaning over the side. With a grumble, Justin began to pull the boat forward as Teddy climbed out to help. The sound of the sand scrapping the bottom of the boat changed in pitch and then finally stopped as the two securely anchored the craft on shore. Taking the lines, Branda leapt gracefully from the bow and ran to tie them to a nearby palm.

"So, this is the Lady's island?" Derek commented, leaping over the side. "Not exactly what I expected."

"And what did you expect? Dancing girls with umbrella'd drinks?" Justin retorted. "This isn't a vacation, Blackwell."

"Obviously. You couldn't afford beach front property."

"Will you two stop?" Cyn Dal stated as she stepped out of the boat, her pack on her shoulder and a large book under her arm.

"I second that," Page added as she followed Cyn Dal.

Taking Teddy's outstretched hand, Elli jumped from the boat, her pack and Justin's heavy on her shoulders. The island's palms fluttered in the breeze that tickled Elli's cheek as she stood on the beach and simply experienced it. The sun was warm on her skin, her toes were curling in the sand, and the sound of her friends unloading the lifeboat behind her was comforting; she wasn't alone. She stood, her back to the ocean, her green eyes taking in the shore of the island she and her friends had traveled so far to see. Though the beach seemed to stretch on for miles in both directions, it was only several yards wide, the sand rushing up to meet the edge of a forest of palms and vines.

Yet, despite the tranquility of her surroundings and the smell of the sea spray as it crashed on the rocks just off shore, Elli felt a creeping feeling of unease that traveled down her arms and made her little fingers tingle. Hauling the packs up onto the beach and dropping them with a thud onto the sand, she moved closer to the dense foliage that lay just beyond the sand's reach.

Elli clenched her fists against the shiver that threatened to crawl up her body. The sound of a soft whine and the feel of a cold nose against her hand made Elli look down. Toby's dark brown eyes looked up at her, almost as if he understood her wariness and wanted to comfort her. Kneeling down beside him to scratch softly behind his ear, Elli's eyes were drawn back to the trees, her unease still prickling through her.

"What's wrong, love?" Justin asked as he came up beside her, dropping a coil of rope and another pack to the ground.

"Don't you feel it?" she questioned, not taking her eyes off the forest as she stood.

"What?"

"The magic. It's so strong that I can almost taste it. But it isn't just that. It's... It's almost wild, like it's been around for so long that it's grown a mind of its own. I can't..." Elli let her voice trail off, unsure of how to explain how the island made her feel almost helpless and yet, at the same, gave off a strange vibe of anticipation like it had been waiting for her, and now that she was here, it couldn't understand why she was stalling on the edge of it. "I can't explain it," she ended lamely, meeting his gray eyes and then quickly looking down.

Elli should have known that she couldn't avoid him that easily. Feeling the gentle touch of his fingertips under her chin, she let him guide her face until their eyes met.

"Maybe we aren't meant to explain it. Maybe we just

have to take it on faith that we're here because we're destined to be." Justin's soft smile and the feel of his hand on her face sent a tremor through Elli that made all the cold, creeping sensations melt at the warmth of his touch. "And whatever we run into in there," he began, breaking eye contact with her only long enough to glance at the forest before meeting her eyes again, "we'll face it together."

"Faith?" Elli began, returning his smile with a teasing one of her own, "That's strange coming from you, the one who's been stubborn about nearly everything up to this point."

"Well, after what we've just been through, can you blame me?"

Brushing her lips across his for the briefest of kisses, Elli replied, "I guess not."

"How sweet," Derek chortled, breaking the moment. Lost in their own conversation, Elli and Justin hadn't heard his approach. "But if you two can pull yourselves away from each other for two seconds, maybe we can figure where we should go next."

"Well, if we're boring you, why don't you just paddle yourself back to the boat?" Justin threw back, running his hand down Elli's arm before taking her hand in his. Derek's eyes grazed their linked hands for only a moment, but the undefinable, fleeting look on his face left a strange feeling in the pit of Elli's stomach that she didn't understand. As quickly as it had come, the expression was gone, and Derek was glaring at Justin.

"Maybe we should check the book," Elli said, stopping the storm before it broke. Without another word, she began walking toward the others who were busy sorting through the supplies, Toby at her heels. Nothing else to do but follow, Justin picked the rope and pack up again, and he and Derek fell into step with her, one on either side. Elli peered at the two as they walked. Their constant fighting left Elli with the sensation of trying to plug the holes in a sinking ship with a single cork. Every time she felt that she had stemmed the rush of incoming water, another hole would burst through the hull.

When they reached the others, Elli plopped down on the sand beside Cyn Dal and pushed her worries over Derek and Justin to the back of her mind because she simply didn't know what to do about them. And yet, while she tried to focus on what was going on around her, she knew with the certainty of a premonition that she was going to have to make a decision that would change everything.

As the others gathered beneath the shade of the palms in various states of relaxation, Elli felt a kind of uneasy silence grow around them. She understood how they felt. Now that they were gathered together on a magic island with Merlin's ancient history book before them, it made the truth of the situation hit home that much harder. They truly were on their own.

"You know," Page began, finally ending the quiet, "this isn't exactly how I pictured a magic island to look. I mean I didn't expect to see gargoyles perched in the trees or unicorns in the serf, but I also didn't expect something this... simple." Page gestured toward the barren beach and the fluttering palms.

"Could it be possible that we're on the wrong island?" Teddy suggested while he leaned closer to Cyn Dal and peered at the pages of the book.

"I find that hard to believe," Branda answered. "I mean there was the waterspout that none of us could tamper with, and all the mechanical problems on the boat afterward. Compasses don't just spin in circles like that without reason."

"Yeah, and not to mention our ship's captain petrifying like that. All put together, I'm pretty sure we're in the right place," Derek added.

"Does the book say anything about where we're supposed to go or what we're supposed to do next?" Elli asked, unsure of whether or not she wanted to share her feelings about the island with the others just yet.

"Not really. It just shows where we are. Look." Cyn Dal placed the book on the sand so they could all see the page. When they had been on the mainland, the book had created a kind of three-dimensional map which had told them the correct direction to travel in. Now the page showed only the shore line of the island and nothing else.

"Don't you think it's kind of strange that the book is only letting us see the general shape of the island and nothing in the middle? I mean if this place was built by the Lady, don't you think she would have given Merlin better directions?" Justin asked.

"You're right," Cyn Dal began, "When we were in England, we could see all around us on the page. Why doesn't it work the same way here? It's like the center of the island has been erased. It isn't even blue like it was when we were on the *Lois Jane*. When it represented water. This is different. It's just blank..."

"What if..." Derek began, letting his voice trail off.

"'What if' what?" Branda asked.

"Nothing," Derek said.

"Come on, Derek," Elli coaxed. "If you think you know what's going on here, say it. Being the strong, silent type isn't going to help us here."

"Well, what if the island is like a false front and what we need to get to is really in the middle."

"I get it," Page began, sitting forward with excitement, "You mean like because we expected to see an island, we see one. The trees and the sand are all fake and the blank middle is the only real thing here."

"Exactly."

Picking up a handful of sand and letting it run through his fingers, Justin spoke, "Only one flaw in that particular theory. I can feel the sand. I can actually feel the grittiness of it. No illusion is that perfect."

"Come on, Spaller," Derek spat, "think! If the Acolytes can make you see what isn't really there, why can't a magic that's infinitely older and more powerful? Besides, since you're used to grubbing in the dirt, you'd already know what it's supposed to feel like."

"Just like you'd know what the Acolytes can do, right?"

Justin seethed.

"Get off my back!" Derek exclaimed, stepping until he was toe-to-toe with Justin, his eyes shining with anger. "You're right. I've done some stupid things and I'm not proud of them, but when is it going to be enough for you to finally trust me?"

"Trust you? Why should I trust you? You not only sided with the enemy, Blackwell, you were Clandestine's right-hand man. You think that by pretending to be a good boy now that I can't see through you. That's crap! I wouldn't trust you any farther than I could throw you." Justin's jaw was set in a tight line, the bone accentuated beneath the skin as he ground his teeth.

"And yet you trusted me enough to take care of Elli during the storm," Derek shot back. The silence that emanated from Justin was so strong that Elli could feel it pulsing even from where she sat. Derek had him, and Justin knew it. Elli barely acknowledged the growl that escaped from Toby's throat, her entire attention focused on the two before her, their forms outlined by the brush behind them.

In a strange, dream-like slow motion, Elli watched Justin's arms connect with Derek's shoulders, shoving him hard. Sand rained down as Derek lost his balance and toppled back, his arms barely having the time to flail. But Derek never connected with the dense brush behind or the grainy sand beneath him. He simply... disappeared.

Release date for the third and final installment of
The Clandestine Series - *The Betrayed* –
Spring/Summer of 2020

Author's Note

As an admirer of literature, I fell in love with Shakespeare and his characters in college. The feisty Katherina of *The Taming of the Shrew*, the trickster Robin Goodfellow in *A Midsummer Night's Dream*, and all their compatriots have, and will always have, a special place in my heart. So, as an ode to my favorite author and his characters, I have used his poetry as an integral part of the fabric of this series.

Made in the USA
Monee, IL
18 April 2024

57174528R00100